CHAPTER ONE

Dylan Walsh took a deep breath, trying to settle her stomach, which seemed to be doing jumping jacks. She rode her pony, Morello, over to the fence of the busy schooling ring, dodging an anxious-looking girl on a fat gray horse as she went.

One of Dylan's best friends, Malory O'Neil, was sitting just outside the ring on a pony named Tybalt. The dark bay Thoroughbred-cross pony's eyes were wide as he took in the show-day action all around him. Nearly a dozen riders were warming up in the schooling ring, trotting and cantering every which way and occasionally popping over the practice jumps.

"Wow," Dylan commented, leaning over to give Morello a quick pat on the neck. "I haven't been this nervous at a show in a long time!"

"I know what you mean." Malory squinted against the

bright late-February sunlight. She looked polished and professional in her royal-blue Chestnut Hill team jacket, gray breeches, and polished black boots. Her long, curly dark hair was tucked up neatly beneath her black velvet safety helmet. "Maybe it's because the show is at *our* school this time. So we've got the pressure of having the hometown crowd."

"That's a plausible theory, Dr. Freud," Dylan joked.

Suddenly, a cheer went up from the direction of Chestnut Hill's main ring. Dylan and Malory turned just in time to see a tall girl on a stocky bay pony ride out through the gate. Most of the spectators crowding the bleachers were clapping politely, but those in the section reserved for visitors from Two Towers Academy were cheering wildly.

"Gee, I wonder who she rides for?" Dylan commented.

Malory put a finger to her chin and pretended to ponder. "Hmm," she said. "She *is* wearing a hunter-green jacket. Do you think she could be from Two Towers?"

Dylan grinned. There were a lot of spectators from the other schools in the athletic league, more than she remembered traveling to previous events. "They're loud," Dylan confirmed. "But our cheering section is still the biggest. That's because our fans are so loyal. Just watch. They'll explode with euphoria when we crush the seven other teams."

"Or maybe they're here because we just got back from

Chestnut Hill

THE SCHEME TEAM

Chestnut Hill

THE SCHEME TEAM

by Lauren Brooke

Ellington Middle School
Library Media Center

SCHOLASTIC INC.
New York Toronto London Auckland Sydney
Mexico City New Delhi Hong Kong Buenos Aires

No part of this publication may be reproduced, stored in a retrieval system, or transmitted in any form or by any means, electronic, mechanical, photocopying, recording, or otherwise, without written permission of the publisher. For information regarding permission, write to Scholastic Inc., Attention: Permissions Department, 557 Broadway, New York, NY 10012.

ISBN 0-439-85998-0

Chestnut Hill series created by Working Partners Ltd, London.

Copyright © 2006 by Working Partners Ltd.
Published by Scholastic Inc. All rights reserved.

SCHOLASTIC and associated logos are trademarks and/or registered trademarks of Scholastic Inc.

12 11 10 9 8 7 6 5 4 3 2 1   6 7 8 9 10 11/0
Printed in the U.S.A.   40
First printing, October 2006

Special thanks to Catherine Hapka

Chestnut Hill

THE SCHEME TEAM

spring break and this is the only thing going on this weekend," Malory pointed out.

Dylan stuck out her tongue. "I like my theory better."

"Dylan! Dylan!"

Dylan saw her and Malory's friends, Honey Harper and Lani Hernandez, hurrying toward the practice ring. They weren't on the junior jumping team, but they always came to the shows to cheer on Dylan and Malory.

"Ms. Carmichael says you're up next," Lani told Dylan. "Better get over there and make sure you're ready."

"Well, here goes nothing." Dylan shortened her pony's reins and headed toward the show ring. Seeing that a rider was still on the course, she glanced around at her friends, who had followed her. "Any last-minute advice before we go in?"

"Make sure you keep him together at the in-and-out," Malory said. "I've been watching, and a lot of people are having trouble there — the striding doesn't allow much room for error."

Lani nodded. "Eleanor and Shamrock were too tight and ate the second element a few rounds ago," she said. "It threw off the whole rest of their course."

"Really? I didn't see her go." Dylan felt a fresh shiver of nerves. Eighth-grader Eleanor Dixon was the captain of the junior jumping team, and her pony was a talented jumper. "So what did that do to our team score?"

"Don't ask." Lani rolled her eyes. "Especially since Olivia and Skylark had some problems, too."

"Yeah." Dylan grimaced, remembering the crestfallen look on Olivia Buckley's face as she'd ridden out of the ring. "That one I saw. Not too pretty."

Honey tucked her shoulder-length blonde hair behind her ear's. "Try not to fret about all that, Dylan," she said in her soft, British-accented voice.

"I know, I know," Dylan said. "We should have it down. Especially since we practiced all kinds of ins-and-outs over the break."

Honey reached out to give Morello a pat on his gleaming pinto neck. "Good. And I'm sure Morello's far too sensible to be scared of that cumbersome new wall jump, too."

"Gee, thanks," Dylan said with mock seriousness. "I'd almost forgotten all about the wall."

"Oh!" Honey's blue eyes widened. "Oh, Dylan, I'm so sorry!"

Dylan laughed at her friend's horrified expression. "Totally kidding," she assured her. "Trust me, I haven't forgotten about it for a second. How could I, after watching Skylark spook like she thought it was a pony-eating monster?" The new wall *was* imposing with its faux red-brick pattern and bulky appearance. It would be an obstacle to reckon with.

"Hey, Walsh, your boots are a mess," Lani put in.

"Ms. C. will disown you if you go in looking like that. Anyone have a rag?"

Honey pulled a scrap of cloth out of her jeans pocket and stepped forward to wipe the dirt off Dylan's boots. "Thanks," Dylan told her, glad that her friends were looking out for her.

"You're up," Lani told Dylan as the previous rider exited the ring. "Knock 'em dead, Walsh!"

As her friends stepped back out of the way, Dylan straightened the chinstrap of her helmet and took another deep breath. "Let's try to stick together out there, okay, Morello?" she said, giving the pony a nudge with her legs. He jumped forward, almost breaking into a trot. Dylan pulled him back with a laugh. "You know what's coming as well as I do, don't you?"

Even though both of them had been in that very ring countless times, it always looked different on show days. The footing had been raked to perfection, the jumps and rails repainted, the obstacles filled in with brush boxes stuffed with evergreen branches or fabric flowers. One obstacle was decorated with gourds, while another featured branches of pussy willows, suggesting the onset of spring. Every jump on the course looked attractive and inviting.

Well, all but one . . .

Despite her best efforts to resist, Dylan's gaze strayed toward the wall as she rode into the ring. Ali Carmichael,

Chestnut Hill's Director of Riding and Dylan's aunt, had warned the students about the new addition to their collection of jumps at the end of last semester, but due to a delay in shipping, it had arrived only the afternoon before. Dylan's first real look at it had been during the course-walk that morning, and she'd been a little surprised by how large and solid it looked compared to the other jumps.

As soon as they cantered through the timers to start their round, Dylan forgot about everything except the course in front of them. Morello's ears flicked forward as he focused on the first jump: a simple vertical consisting of a couple of poles over a small flower box filled with daffodils.

Three, two, one . . . Dylan didn't have to adjust Morello's stride at all as the pony found the perfect spot and arced easily over the fence, his polished hooves clearing the top rail by several inches.

Dylan smiled as Morello let out a small buck upon landing. But she quickly kicked him on, focusing her attention on the next jump, another vertical. Usually she enjoyed the spirited pony's high jinks, but today they needed to stay focused.

Morello sped up a little at Dylan's urging, and they met the second fence a little short. But the pony was an athletic jumper, and he managed to round himself over the top rail without touching it. When he landed, Dylan sat up and half-halted, getting control of his stride again. Morello responded well, and they made it over the third and fourth jumps with no trouble.

Next came the in-and-out, which consisted of a two-vertical set only two strides apart. With the need for exact striding and incredible athleticism, ins-and-outs were always a challenge. As they cantered toward it, Malory's advice rang in Dylan's ears. But Dylan wasn't too worried. She and Morello had schooled through a similar in-and-out just a few days earlier. In fact, they'd had all the jumps at Chestnut Hill to themselves for the past two weeks during the school's spring break. Normally Dylan would have gone home to Connecticut, but her parents were spending February and March traveling in Europe. Although they'd invited her to join them, Dylan had opted instead to remain on campus with her aunt.

It had been fun to spend some family time with Ali — it was sometimes difficult trying to separate the fun-loving aunt she'd known all her life from the strict but fair Director of Riding who expected all her students, including Dylan, to address her as Ms. Carmichael. Ali had asked Dylan to help her and the stable hands keep the horses and ponies exercised, which meant Dylan had ridden at least five or six ponies every single day for two weeks — always including Morello, of course. Morello belonged to her aunt, along with a spirited Thoroughbred cross named Quince, and the two of them had joined the Chestnut Hill school string when Ali had taken over the Riding Director job at the beginning of the school year. Dylan couldn't have been luckier. Morello was the perfect pony for her — in size and in his wily personality.

Quickly sizing up the distance to the first fence of the combination, Dylan realized they were coming in too fast. She sat back and half-halted with a squeeze of the reins, and the well-trained pony responded immediately, collecting his stride. Morello jumped into the combination strongly but roundly, which allowed him to fit in two neat strides before powering out over the second fence.

"Good boy!" Dylan shouted, reaching forward to give him a quick pat on the neck.

The next several jumps flashed by in what felt like a matter of seconds. Before she knew it, Dylan found herself cantering toward the wall.

A flock of butterflies seemed to skitter through her stomach. But she banished them quickly. *Focus,* she told herself. *It's just another jump.*

But Morello had sensed her brief moment of nerves. She felt him hesitate beneath her, his stride faltering slightly.

She sat down and drove him on. For a second she thought it wouldn't be enough — at this rate, they would meet the imposing wall on a half stride, which could lead to a chip or even a refusal. Dylan held her breath.

But Morello seemed to sense what was needed. He surged forward in a bouncy canter, meeting the wall a hair short, but powering over it without hesitation. As they landed, Dylan didn't even bother to listen for the sound of the top row of faux bricks hitting the ground. She knew they'd cleared it.

There were only two fences after that. Not allowing herself to let up, Dylan steered Morello over them for a clear round — the first of the day for Chestnut Hill's junior team. Dylan grinned and gave Morello a hearty pat.

"That was brilliant, Dylan!" Honey's eyes were shining as she hurried forward to meet them outside the gate. "Absolutely brilliant!"

"Thanks!" Dylan dropped the reins on Morello's neck and leaned forward to give the pony a hug. "Morello was awesome! And I must say, I was feeling a little Beezie Maddenish myself," Dylan added, referencing one of the top professionals on the U.S. team. "Guess all our practice over spring break paid off."

"Awesome job, Dylan! Way to go!"

Dylan turned and saw Eleanor and Olivia waving to her from nearby, along with several older students from the intermediate jumping team, who would be riding when the junior competition finished. With a grin, Dylan returned the wave.

"Thanks, guys!" she called.

Lani reached out to grab Morello's reins as Dylan swung down from the saddle. "Allow *me*, Beezie," she said with a mock bow. "I'll play groom and walk him out if you want to watch a few rounds."

"That's okay," Dylan said as she loosened her pony's girth. "I don't mind walking him."

"No, no." Lani waggled a finger at her. "A star rider like you always has grooms to take care of the grunt work."

Dylan grinned. "Okay, if you insist," she said, unbuckling her helmet. When she pulled it off, her thick red hair immediately burst free of its bobby pins and hairnet. "Thanks, Lani," she added, picking the hairnet out of her hair and sticking it in her jacket pocket. Then she rubbed her temples, feeling the hint of a headache starting. Maybe it was time to hit up her parents for a new, more comfortable helmet. . . . "Oh, and how about bringing me a lemonade and some M&M's while you're at it?" she called out as Lani turned away. "But make sure you pick out all of the blue ones!"

Chapter Two

Dylan and Honey wandered back toward the rail. They were just in time to watch the next rider, a nervous-looking seventh-grader wearing the navy and white of Lindenwood Country Day School, ride into the ring on a short-necked chestnut pony.

"Nice riding, Dylan." Ansty Van Sweetering, a freshman member of the intermediate team, greeted the two seventh-graders with a smile. Ansty's pale-blonde hair was already tucked up under her Charles Owen helmet, and her long, slim legs were encased in Tailored Sportsman breeches and custom boots.

"Thanks," Dylan said. "Morello was awesome, wasn't he?"

Eleventh-graders Colette Prior and Kelsey Howett were leaning on the ring fence nearby. Though both girls were in the advanced riding class, only Kelsey was on the senior jumping team.

"Yeah, you guys did great," Kelsey told Dylan with a smile.

"No wonder," Colette said in a mock whisper that Dylan was pretty sure was meant to be loud enough for her to hear. "She's the only one of us who got much riding in over break. How ridiculous is it that Ms. Carmichael expects people to ride in this show three days after we get back?"

"I know!" A junior from Granville dorm turned to join in the conversation. Like Colette, Clare Houlder was an advanced rider but had not made the senior team this year. "I spent two weeks lounging on the beach in Mexico. I could barely make it through our riding class on Thursday without my legs falling off. No wonder the junior team isn't doing that well."

Dylan frowned. Hadn't Clare just seen her lay down a clear round?

A talkative Curie House sophomore named Jessica Jones, who was a member of the intermediate team, leaned over to join the conversation. "It's even more embarrassing to mess up when we're hosting the show," she said. "I mean, I have friends at Allbrights and Two Towers — they're never going to let me live it down if they slaughter us today on our home turf."

"Yeah," Clare agreed. "Too bad Ms. Carmichael didn't think about that before she agreed to this show date."

Dylan's temper flared at that, and she couldn't take being on the outskirts of the conversation a second more. "Look, it's not Ms. Carmichael's fault," she spoke up. "The schedule was set by the league ages ago. They must not have realized our spring break fell when it did. Besides, you knew the meet was coming — you could have taken time to prepare over break."

The older girls turned to stare at her in surprise. "Well, Ms. Carmichael should have told them as soon as she realized," Clare said. "It's in the league's interest that all teams perform their best."

Dylan opened her mouth to answer. But just then she felt Honey touch her on the arm and then give a tug when Dylan didn't respond.

"It's okay," Honey murmured, too softly for the others to hear. "They're just letting off steam 'cause they're nervous."

"Nervous about what?" Dylan muttered, glaring at the older girls, who had already turned away and were continuing their complaints among themselves. "Clare and Colette aren't on the team. They aren't even riding today!"

"Still, it's not worth getting upset over," Honey advised. "Let it go."

Dylan rolled her eyes. In her opinion, Honey could sometimes be a little too quick to "let things go." She turned away, hoping to distract herself by focusing on the pair in the ring. The Lindenwood rider's nervous look had faded, replaced by determination. The girl rode neatly over the last few jumps of the course, including the wall, and finished with a clear round.

"Check it out," Jessica said brightly. "Lynsey's next. She'll bring up the junior team score if anyone can."

So what was my round, chopped liver? Dylan wondered with a flash of irritation. Her snobby roommate Lynsey Harrison loved to remind everyone who would listen how accomplished and/or lucky she was in just about everything she attempted — riding, academics, and field hockey, not to mention her obvious luck in the realm of looks, wealth, and boys. It drove Dylan crazy. However, even Dylan had to admit that Lynsey *was* a good rider, especially when paired with her own flashy blue roan pony, Bluegrass, who had won tri-colored champion ribbons at A shows all up and down the East Coast.

Lynsey rode into the ring with her custom-made Vogel boots polished to a sheen and her blonde hair neatly tucked up under the latest model GPA helmet. With the help of Lynsey's doting friend Patience, Bluegrass had been clipped, bathed, and braided within an inch of his life, and could have stepped into the Dixon Oval at Devon without looking out of place.

The first several jumps looked as smooth and effortless as a round at Devon, too. Even though she was watching carefully, Dylan couldn't see any adjustments at all as the pair approached the in-and-out. Bluegrass simply flowed over it, neatly tucking up his front hooves as he cleared the first fence, then jumping back out over the second as calmly and easily as if it were a simple cross rail. The next few jumps went just as well.

Dylan realized she was holding her breath as Lynsey and Bluegrass cantered toward the wall. Bluegrass's head went up and his ears pricked as he took a hard look at the unfamiliar jump.

"Get up!" Lynsey called to her pony, her voice carrying to the hushed crowd along the rail. Bluegrass responded by leaping up and over the wall, clearing it by at least six inches.

"Way to go, Lyns!" Clare cheered, bursting into applause even though the course wasn't over yet. Others were clapping as well, and Dylan could see a grin spreading across Lynsey's face as she turned Bluegrass toward the second-to-last jump, a square oxer.

"Watch it, watch it," Dylan muttered as she saw the pony's stride flatten.

Lynsey's grin disappeared and she fiddled with her reins, trying to adjust Bluegrass's stride.

But it was too late. Bluegrass tried to take off from an impossibly awkward spot. He lifted both forefeet off the ground but twisted to the side, skidding into the fence for a refusal.

"Wow," Dylan said. "I don't think I've ever seen Bluegrass stop before!"

Lynsey gave her pony a sharp rap on the hindquarters with her crop. Bluegrass hopped in place, his nostrils flaring.

Honey winced. "Poor Bluegrass," she murmured.

Dylan nodded. "The refusal was Lynsey's fault, not his," she said. "She's lucky he had the sense to stop instead of just crashing through it."

On course, Lynsey circled the pony and aimed him at the oxer again. This time Bluegrass jumped it, though his stride was choppy and he took off too close. As he lurched up and over, his hind legs caught the front rail, bringing it to the ground.

"Oh, no!" Jessica cried. "That's four faults, plus the refusal."

Honey shook her head sadly. "She was doing so well, too."

"She got overconfident." Dylan was disappointed that Lynsey's round wouldn't be much help for the team score, but she couldn't avoid a tiny glimmer of satisfaction at seeing Miss Perfect make a mistake. "It's like Ms. Carmichael always tells us — every fence counts. We have to ride to every one, even the ones we think are going to be easy."

She watched as Bluegrass cleared the final fence in his usual good form. Lynsey was scowling as she rode toward the gate. She dismounted as soon as she was out-side and stomped off toward the barn with Bluegrass trailing behind her. Dylan frowned, annoyed by Lynsey's attitude. The least she could do was give her pony a pat.

Just then Lani appeared. "Hey," she greeted Dylan and Honey. "What'd I miss?"

Dylan was surprised to see her. "You seem to be miss-ing a pony," she said. "Where's Morello? He can't be cooled down already."

"Nope," Lani said. "But I found a substitute barn ser-vant. I heard the announcer say that Mal was on deck and I didn't want to miss her round. Emily volunteered to finish walking Morello and hose him off for you."

Dylan nodded. Emily Page was a seventh-grade basic rider who sometimes rode Morello in her lessons. Dylan wasn't always crazy about how Emily rode the pony, but she knew she could handle cooling him out.

"Excellent," she said. "I don't want to miss Malory's ride, either." She held up her hand, showing her friends her crossed fingers. "I just hope Tybalt doesn't freak out when he gets a look at the course."

Tybalt was still fairly new to Chestnut Hill, having arrived late in the fall semester. He had an uncertain his-tory and was more high-strung than most of the other school horses, and sometimes he could be spooky and tense in new situations. Malory possessed an uncanny skill for reading horses and she had been working with him over the past couple of months. He was starting to trust her more and more. But when it came to the hectic, unpredictable atmosphere of a show, all the girls knew there were no guarantees that Tybalt's recent training would overcome his nervous temperament.

Honey nodded. "Especially the new wall," she said. She held up her crossed fingers next to Dylan's. "But if anyone can do it, it's Malory."

They all turned to watch as Malory rode into the ring. Tybalt spooked at the timer flags, but Malory sat quietly through it, then steered him toward the first jump. She gave the sensitive gelding her usual tactful ride, and Tybalt responded by clearing every fence as if he'd been doing it for years. When they made the turn toward the wall, Tybalt skittered a few steps to one side, clearly nervous about the unusual-looking obstacle. But Malory quietly urged him forward. He left long and overjumped, but he got over it. They finished the course with a clear round, the second of the day for Chestnut Hill.

"Awesome job!" Lani cried, letting out an enthusiastic whoop. She grabbed Dylan's arm with one hand and Honey's with the other. "Come on, guys — let's go meet her at the gate."

They pushed their way through the crowd and arrived just as Malory exited the ring. "You were amazing!" Dylan told her, walking beside Tybalt's shoulder as Malory rode the pony away from the congested gate area.

"Thanks." Malory sounded breathless as she dismounted and gave Tybalt a fond pat. "Can you believe how well he handled everything? I thought I might be asking too much of him with that wall at this point in his training, but he was up for it. I'm so proud of him!"

Dylan grinned. Malory wasn't much of a talker under most circumstances. But once you got her going about horses — especially Tybalt — look out!

"Well, we're proud of *you*," Lani said, grabbing Malory and giving her a hug. "Now come on, we'll help you cool him off."

"Okay, let's — no, wait!" Dylan interrupted herself. "What about Caleb? He's riding soon. And I'm sure Mal doesn't want to miss cheering him on, right Mal?"

Dylan took every opportunity she could to mention Caleb in Malory's company. Malory had met Caleb Smith at her local stable the summer before starting at Chestnut Hill. He was in eighth grade at Saint Christopher's Academy, better known at Saint Kits. At first Malory had insisted he was just a friend. But after several weekend outings and casually hanging out at school dances, Malory was no longer denying the fact that there might be a mutual attraction. Dylan was glad she was coming around, because in her opinion, Malory and Caleb might as well be in the dictionary under "perfect couple."

Malory was blushing as Lani and Honey traded grins.

"I don't know," Malory said. "I need to take care of Tybalt."

Even if Malory wouldn't admit it, Dylan was sure her friend wanted to watch Caleb ride. It was riding that had brought them together in the first place, and Caleb was almost as good in the saddle as Malory was. That was one reason they were so good together. Besides, Dylan hated to see anything get in the way of true love.

"I have a fab idea," she said. "Tybalt can cool down walking around out here just as well as anywhere, right? Plus, it'll help him adjust to all of the commotion of being at a show."

Lani laughed. "You're a genius, Dylan. Give me the saddle — I'll run it inside and bring out his cooler."

It was the perfect solution. They helped Malory walk Tybalt up and down the paths while one more Two Towers rider and one from Alice Allbright's School for Girls rode their rounds.

After that, it was Caleb's turn. He was the last rider of the day. He looked handsome in his dark riding jacket with the Saint Christopher's classic gold crest, and his horse, Pageant's Pride — better known around the barn as Gent — was easy on the eyes as well.

They performed as well as they looked, laying down a clean trip without a single bobble. Gent didn't even flick an ear at the wall, sailing over it easily.

"Wow, that was awesome," Lani said, watching as

Caleb rode out of the ring and was mobbed by his excited teammates.

Honey nodded. "The whole St. Kits team rode really well today."

"Don't remind us!" Dylan said. "I'm afraid to hear the final team scores. Come on, let's go congratulate Caleb."

Dylan led her friends as they pushed their way through the crowds of happy St. Kits boys around Caleb, reaching him just as he swung down from the saddle. "Hi!" he greeted them, still breathing hard from his round. He pulled off his helmet and ran a hand through his brown hair, making it stick up in all directions.

"You and Gent looked great out there," Dylan said. "Right, Mal?" She elbowed Malory in the ribs.

"Yeah," Malory said. "Really great." Malory looked at the ground as she said the words, but her voice was genuine.

"Thanks," Caleb said.

Dylan grinned. She couldn't help noticing that although Caleb was supposed to be addressing both of them, he seemed to only acknowledge Malory. Dylan was still smiling to herself about that when she heard the PA system crackle to life.

"Attention, please," Ms. Carmichael announced. "I have the results of the junior team competition. The winner is . . ."

Dylan held her breath. *Okay, so our team didn't do perfectly today,* she thought hopefully. *But Mal and I had clear rounds, and Lynsey didn't do too badly, so maybe, just maybe . . .*

". . . Saint Christopher's," Ms. Carmichael finished.

Dylan let out her breath in a whoosh as Caleb grinned and pumped his fist in the air. "Awesome!" he exclaimed, trading high fives with several of his teammates. "We did it!"

"In second place," Ms. Carmichael continued, "we have Alice Allbright's School for Girls. And in third place are your hosts, Chestnut Hill Academy."

Dylan groaned. "Oh, man," she said as Ms. Carmichael announced the rest of the placings. "It's bad enough to come in third at home. But did we really have to lose to Allbright's? They'll rub it in all season!"

"Hey, what about us?" Caleb joked as he loosened Gent's girth. "Shouldn't you resent us for beating you, too?"

"Of course," Dylan said. "Just not as much. You're not our biggest rival in everything. You *are* an all-boys school, remember?"

She glanced over toward the Allbright's team. They were over near their school's horse trailers, gathered around their Director of Riding. Elizabeth Mitchell had held the same job at Chestnut Hill until receiving a better offer from the rival school at the end of the previous year.

"Ms. Mitchell's done a great job with that team in just one year," Caleb commented. "There's no shame in being beaten by them."

"Speak for yourself," Dylan muttered.

"Oh, well." Malory sounded more philosophical, as usual. "Third place isn't so bad. It gives us something to improve on next time, right?"

"Right!" Honey agreed. "Besides, you two should be proud of yourselves regardless — you were both fantastic!"

"Thanks everyone, for coming today," Ms. Carmichael continued over the PA system. "The intermediate team competition will start in just a moment. But now, I have an announcement. The eight Directors of Riding have finished voting for the first of today's three Equitation Awards. As you all know, these awards go to the best overall rider at the show in each age group — and today for the junior riders, our winner is Caleb Smith from Saint Christopher's."

Dylan let out a whoop. "Way to go, Caleb!"

Malory impulsively grabbed Caleb and gave him a hug. Dylan raised her eyebrows, amused by the very un-Malory-like public display of affection. Suddenly seeming to realize that everyone was watching, Malory quickly pulled away.

"Um, congratulations," she said, turning bright red as several of Caleb's teammates let out whistles.

"Thanks." Caleb looked just as red as Malory did. He gave her a shy smile. "I'd better go walk Gent now. See you later." He glanced around the group quickly before scurrying off with his horse following along.

"Good for Caleb," Lani said, as the four friends headed toward the Chestnut Hill stables. "It's about time he was recognized for his talents. Well, other than that Best Kisser in the World award Malory gave him. Right, Mal?"

"Be quiet! You know we haven't . . ." Malory began before cutting herself off, belatedly realizing that Lani had only been teasing.

Dylan grinned at Honey, who also looked amused. Just then a voice suddenly cut through the chatter all around them.

"Too bad someone from Chestnut Hill couldn't have won Best Junior Rider," a girl said with a bitter laugh. "But I guess that wasn't a remote possibility today, was it?"

Dylan glanced around quickly to see who had said it, but all she saw was a flash of blonde hair before the speaker was hidden by the shifting crowds. *What was that all about?* Dylan wondered. *She and Malory had ridden perfectly well.*

Then she shrugged off the thought. The show was too much fun to let it be spoiled by someone else's bad attitude. Dylan's moment of disappointment over the placings had passed, and she was already looking forward to cheering on Chestnut Hill's intermediate and senior teams.

"Come on," she said to her friends. "Let's go finish taking care of the ponies so we can get back out there and watch the rest of the show!"

CHAPTER THREE

Inside the barn, Dylan headed immediately toward Morello's stall at the end of the aisle beside the tack room. Emily was just pulling off his cooler.

"I think he's all cooled off now," she told Dylan. "I walked him and let him graze a little."

"Cool. Thanks a million for taking care of him, Emily," Dylan said. "I totally owe you one."

Emily smiled. "Then you can take my next turn on tack-cleaning duty."

"Deal." Dylan gave her a wave as she wandered off, then let herself into Morello's stall. The pony was munching on a large pile of hay, but he pricked his ears when he heard the familiar rustle of Dylan's carrot bag.

"You were a superstar today, buddy," Dylan told him as she offered a chunk of carrot. "Totally awesome."

As Morello crunched quickly through the carrot,

Dylan checked him over and picked up his feet. Emily had done a good job — the pony was spotless. After giving him a pat and another piece of carrot, Dylan ducked out under the stall guard.

Honey was standing in front of a stall a few doors down from Morello's. A pretty gray pony was hanging her head out over the door, her soft brown eyes half closed as Honey scratched under her forelock.

"I wonder if Minnie wishes she could be in the show today," Honey said.

The stylish pony's show name was Moonlight Minuet, and she was owned by Lynsey Harrison's best friend, Patience Duvall. As a member of the basic riding class, Patience was an indifferent rider at best. Dylan and her friends had all been surprised to learn that Patience had gotten her own pony that year —especially a pony as spectacular as Minnie. Although Minnie was good-natured and beautifully trained, her lofty gaits and big jump had given Patience trouble from the start. And after Patience and Lynsey had strained Minnie's tendons by working her too hard in deep, wet sand, Patience had totally lost interest in her pony. She wasn't invested enough to spend time helping Minnie heal, but Honey had been. Honey had felt an immediate connection to the mare, and she still did — especially after weeks of wrapping her sore legs and eventually leading her on walks. Patience's wealthy novelist father had agreed to keep Minnie at Chestnut Hill to be used as a school pony until Patience decided whether she wanted to keep her.

Malory stuck her head out of Tybalt's stall. "I don't think Minnie's ready to start jumping courses yet," she said. "I overheard Ms. Carmichael say that her tendons are pretty well healed, but I think she just started her back to work. Right, Dylan?"

"Right," Dylan said. "Over break, I saw Sarah and Kelly lunging her. She looked really great. All her gaits were long and smooth. She must be an incredible ride."

Just then they all heard the clatter of hooves at the far end of the aisle. Dylan saw that Jessica Jones had just led her mount, a petite part-Arabian mare named Foxy Lady, into the barn.

"Hey!" Dylan called to the older girl, realizing that Jessica must have just finished her round for the intermediate team. "How'd it go?"

Jessica scowled. "She refused the very first jump, then knocked it down. And she practically turned herself inside out at that stupid wall."

"Sorry," Dylan said sympathetically. She glanced at the mare, who looked sweaty and tired. Jessica was a strong rider, but she could be a little tense at times, which didn't always mesh well with Foxy's sensitive temperament.

Jessica shrugged and disappeared with Foxy into the

wash stall, clearly not in the mood for further conversation. Dylan wandered over toward Lani, who had just ducked into Colorado's stall. The spunky buckskin was Lani's favorite mount — not only was his name the same as her home state, but he could go just as well in either English or Western, just like Lani herself.

"We'd better get back out there and see what's happening," Dylan said. "It sounds like we're missing some, um, interesting action."

Lani gave Colorado a pat. "Let's go."

The four girls reached the ring just in time to see Chestnut Hill freshman Paige Rivers go clear on her own horse, a strawberry roan Appaloosa-cross named Hopeful Rose. But that turned out to be the highlight of the day for the hosting team on the intermediate level. Jillian Watt and Ansty each knocked down multiple rails, and Sophie Chatterton's mount, a normally placid bay gelding named Gandalf, got himself eliminated by refusing the wall three times. By the time the last intermediate rider finished, the entire Chestnut Hill cheering section was silent and dejected.

Dylan sighed and looked at her friends. Things felt very tense in the bleachers, and she was about to suggest they hit the concession stand when she heard a hushed voice come from the row behind them.

"Well, I'm not surprised! Ms. Carmichael should not

have put the wall out today. Our horses never got a chance to get acclimated to it. Why weren't they schooled over it during spring break?"

Dylan glanced over her shoulder to see Clare Houlder sitting there with a sour look on her face.

"Well, I heard the wall just arrived, so there wasn't really any time for that," Jillian explained.

Clare rolled her eyes and waved off Jillian's comment. "Then she shouldn't have used the wall. Plain and simple. When I was intermediate team captain last year, Ms. Mitchell always had us school over every possible type of obstacle. That way the horses went into the ring looking like seasoned competitors, not backyard trail ponies."

"You were intermediate captain last year?" Dylan blurted out without thinking. "So why aren't you on the senior team this year?"

Clare glared at Dylan at first. It wasn't appropriate social protocol for an underclasswoman to invite herself into a junior's conversation. "Well," Clare said icily, "maybe if Ms. Carmichael would have let me keep riding Snapdragon instead of throwing me onto Sancha two weeks before tryouts . . ." She let her voice trail off meaningfully before turning back to address Jillian again. "Anyway, it stinks that we had to lose a Riding Director with so much experience and talent. Allbright's totally lucked out when Ms. Mitchell went over there."

Now that her brain had caught up to her mouth, Dylan remembered hearing some barn gossip about Clare's horse switch. The eleventh-grader had been riding Snapdragon, a large pony, since arriving at Chestnut Hill as a seventh-grader. However, during the past four years Clare had shot up to a willowy five foot nine, and one of the first things Ali had done was switch her over to Sancha, a wide-bodied sixteen-hand quarter horse.

"Yeah, right, Clare," Dylan said. "I'm sure the mighty and glorious Ms. Mitchell would still have you riding Snapdragon. That way you wouldn't have to worry about him knocking down the jumps — you could just kick them over yourself, since your feet would be hanging two feet below his —"

"Hey!" Lani elbowed Dylan in the ribs, interrupting her. Her eyes were flared in warning. "The jump crew is setting the fences for the senior course. Let's go help out."

Dylan took the hint. She could only get herself into more trouble if she stuck around. "Right behind you," she replied. She hurried off, ignoring Clare's glare.

ᕮ᠀

"Wow, that guy is good," Malory commented to Dylan.

She was leaning on the ring fence, her eyes glued to a senior team member from Lindenwood and his lanky chestnut Thoroughbred. Lani and Honey were on

Dylan's other side, also watching the action in the ring. In fact, most of Chestnut Hill's junior and intermediate team members were gathered at the fence, still dressed in their breeches and boots as they watched the eleventh- and twelfth-grade riders compete. To Dylan's dismay, Clare Houlder was there, too, along with her best friends and fellow advanced riders Colette Prior and Chloe Bates. The three juniors were inseparable and had earned the shared nickname of the "Three C's."

"Heads up — Kelsey and Snapdragon are next," Jillian commented from a little farther down the rail.

"Uh-oh," Honey said, glancing over. Snapdragon was prancing like a parade horse, his dark gray legs flying, as Kelsey tried to steer him through the gate. "Looks like they're both feeling kind of nervous."

"Is that pony spooking at the gate?" Lynsey wondered out loud. She was standing farther down the rail with Patience, who looked bored. "He only sees it every day!"

"He's picking up on Kelsey's nerves." Malory was watching the pair closely. "See how his ears keep flicking back? He's checking with his rider to see if there's anything to be scared of."

Dylan was impressed as always with Malory's insights into equine behavior. But at the moment she was more interested in seeing Chestnut Hill turn in a decent performance to make up for the mediocre showing of the two younger teams.

"Come on, Kels," she chanted. "You can do it."

"Don't count on it," Clare said from her spot on the rail on Malory's other side. "Snapdragon can be a fantastic jumper with the right rider. But with Kelsey?" She shrugged and traded a smirk with Colette. "She's too rigid in the ring. . . ."

Dylan blinked, surprised by the older girl's snarky comments. She had thought Clare and Kelsey were friends.

"Way to show your team spirit," she spoke up, suddenly feeling the need to defend Kelsey, since she wasn't there to defend herself. "Can't you at least pretend you want to see Kelsey and Snap do well?"

She heard a sharp intake of breath beside her. "Easy," Honey murmured. It wasn't often that a seventh-grader mouthed off to an upperclassman without living to regret it.

But Clare barely glanced over at her. "Whatever, Dylan," she said. "I'm just being realistic. That's probably a concept that's a little over the head of someone your age."

Dylan was about to point out which of the two of them was making immature comments, but just then Malory elbowed her. "She's starting," she said, nodding toward the ring.

Kelsey had just pushed Snapdragon into a canter. The gray gelding picked up the wrong lead, then tossed his head and humped his back. Kelsey's face, which was pale as a sheet, started to go pink. She tapped Snapdragon with her crop, and the pony sprang forward, ears pinned.

"I don't think she realizes she's still on the wrong lead," Lani commented.

Dylan nodded, biting her lip. The pony was clearly off balance. "Snap's a pro," she said. "He could make it around that course without a rider if he had to."

"You may think that," Clare broke in again. "But that pony isn't as easy as I made him look.

"Come on, Clare," Jillian put in. "That's not fair. Snap was a successful show pony before he came here. And Kelsey has been doing pretty well with him so far this year."

Just then there was a clatter of rails hitting the ground. Glancing out into the ring, Dylan winced as she saw that Snapdragon had knocked down the top two rails of the first fence.

"Oh, really?" Clare pursed her lips. "If *that's* what you call 'doing well' . . ."

As if on cue, Snapdragon's front hooves clattered against the next obstacle, pulling off the top rail. Dylan felt sorry for Kelsey. She had been there herself — sometimes a round was just a disaster from the first fence.

The pair managed to make it around the next part of the course without any more faults, though Snapdragon did nick several rails. But as the pony approached the wall, everything looked off kilter.

Snapdragon took one look at the bright red blocks and leaped to one side. Kelsey was nearly unseated, but she quickly regrouped and turned the gelding toward the obstacle again.

On the second try, Snapdragon bulged his shoulder and ducked out again. Kelsey aimed the gelding at the wall once more, but it was no use. The pony had decided he wasn't going near the fence, and this time he planted his front feet and tossed in a small buck to prove it.

"Eliminated," Clare said succinctly as Kelsey slumped in her saddle and allowed Snapdragon to stroll toward the gate.

"You don't have to sound so *happy* about it," Dylan said. "If you understand Snapdragon so well, maybe you should share your insight with Kelsey."

"Why should I help her look better than she is?" Clare shrugged. "If she's good enough to be on the team, she should be good enough to figure him out. That's what I did, and I won all sorts of ribbons on him."

"Well, congratulations," Dylan muttered.

"Shhh," Honey whispered. "Forget her. It's just sour grapes 'cause she didn't make the senior team this year."

Dylan nodded. She forgot all about the catty older girls a couple of rounds later when Sara Chappell and

Mischief Maker came into the ring. "Ooh," she breathed, taking in Mischief's gleaming bay coat and polished black hooves. Sara was Dylan's favorite of the senior riders, and she was also cocaptain of the team. "They look ready to take care of business."

Mischief swung into a ground-covering canter and headed for the first fence. Sara sat quietly, her position in the saddle impeccable and her eyes trained calmly ahead. Dylan held her breath, watching as the gelding took off from the perfect spot, tucking his knees up almost to his chin as he cleared the fence easily.

"Wow," Dylan said. "They're incred —"

She broke off with a gasp as the gelding bobbled awkwardly on the first stride away from the fence. He threw up his head, immediately switching leads in front and cross-cantering a few steps.

"What's wrong?" Honey cried.

"I don't know." Malory was clutching the rail as she watched. "Something happened when he landed."

Dylan watched, her heart in her throat, as Sara circled out from the course line and brought Mischief Maker down to a trot. Each time the gelding's front left hoof hit the ground, his head bobbed and his nostrils flared.

"Not good," Lani said. "He went from perfectly sound to totally lame with one jump! What do you think it was?"

Sara had brought Mischief to a halt and dismounted.

She was leading him out of the ring toward the barn, her face pinched in a mask of anxiety.

"Come on." Dylan couldn't bear to stand around speculating when one of her favorite horses could be badly hurt. "Let's go back to the barn and see what the vet says."

CHAPTER FOUR

The rest of the afternoon dragged by for Dylan. The accident with Mischief Maker put a damper on the day, and Dylan felt like she was barely able to get herself back to the dorm after the end of the senior team competition. She definitely felt a headache coming on.

Adams House was a rush of excitement as all of the riding students prepared for the postshow party, yet Dylan was not looking forward to it as much as usual — not even for the opportunity to tease Malory and Caleb in person.

"Get a grip, Dylan," she told herself, but the dull pain in her head made it impossible to feel festive. It didn't help that the hum of her hair dryer seemed to be in perfect sync with the throbbing in her sinuses.

Dylan switched off her blow-dryer. "Hey, does anyone have some Tylenol?" she asked her friends, who were all in her dorm room primping for the party.

"Why? Did you bake your brain with that thing?" Lani joked, glancing up from Honey's makeup mirror. "I told you don't dry your hair on the extra-crispy setting."

Honey laughed. "I'm sure you can get Tylenol from Ms. Herson," she told Dylan. "Do you have a headache?"

"Sort of." It wasn't Dylan's style to admit any ailment. "But it's no big deal. I'm not about to miss out on an All Schools social event. Come on, how often do we see boys around here? Is there anyone you might want to chat with tonight, Mal?" Dylan paused for a moment and then turned to Malory with a coy smile. "This party will be a great chance for conversation."

"Shut up," Malory said, though she was smiling as she said it.

"Too bad Josh isn't on the riding team," Lani added, winking at Dylan.

Josh was Caleb's friend from St. Kits. He and Honey had met during a weekend trip into the nearby town of Cheney Falls and struck up a friendship that seemed on its way to becoming something more.

"Definitely too bad," Dylan agreed. "Otherwise Honey might be able to strike up a conversation tonight, too. As it is, she might have to wait until the Spring Fling dance at St. Kits in a couple of weeks. Now Honey, it's not going to be easy living up to Mal and Caleb's reputation as the most adorable perfect couple in the entire state of Virginia, but all you and Josh can do is try your best."

"Forget the state of Virginia," Lani put in as she dabbed at her dark lashes with a mascara wand. "Mal and Caleb are going for the national title."

"I stand corrected." Dylan grinned. "But I still think Honey and Josh can give them some competition at the Fling if they try really hard.

Honey blushed. "Would you guys stop it?" she said. "We'd better hurry up or we'll miss the whole party."

"You guys go ahead," Dylan said. "I'm going to stop off at Hersie's suite for some Tylenol. I'll be there soon."

When she arrived in the cafeteria fifteen minutes later, the place was packed with students chattering, drinking cups of punch, and snacking on the chips, cookies, and other treats on the long buffet table at one end of the room. Most of the visiting riders were still wearing at least part of their riding outfits, though almost all the Chestnut Hill girls had changed into other clothes. They had to wear uniforms to class, which meant most of them were eager for any opportunity to dress up and look fashionable.

One of the first people Dylan encountered was Patience, who was standing near the entrance talking to a cute dark-haired guy from Lindenwood. "Nice riding today, Dylan," she called out.

Dylan was so shocked by the pleasant words that she stopped short. She couldn't remember the last time

Patience had complimented her. In fact, she was pretty sure Patience had *never* complimented her. They had been at odds since the second week of school.

"Um . . . thanks?" she said cautiously.

The Lindenwood guy peered at her. "Hey, you were the one on the pinto pony, right?" he said. "That pony rules! I remember him from the last All Schools show."

Dylan smiled, wondering why such an obviously smart and discerning guy was wasting his time talking to Patience. "His name's Morello. He belongs to Ms. Carmichael, but she uses him as a school pony."

"Yeah. But only for *certain* students." Patience smirked and tossed her head, making her glossy, chin-length dark hair bounce. "Dylan sort of forgot to mention that Ms. Carmichael is her aunt. So that means Dylan gets the best pony to ride and extra practice over spring break to make her look good."

That sounded more like the Patience Dylan knew. "Well, we can't all have our rich daddies buy us fabulous ponies that we can't ride," she said airily, deciding it was time to move on. The Tylenol hadn't kicked in yet, and talking to Patience would only make her headache worse. "See you around." She added to Patience's companion. "Oh, and thanks for being so nice to Patience. We'll make sure you get community-service points for your time."

She hurried away, disappearing into the crowd to the

sound of Patience's murmurs of disgust. After a few minutes of searching, Dylan managed to locate her friends over near the food tables.

"There you are!" Lani greeted her. "You missed all the fun — we were just eavesdropping on the Allbright's team." She grinned. "I'm not sure they realize they're at a party. They were all discussing the tips Ms. Mitchell had given them for ways to do better next time."

"Do better?" Dylan said. "But they did great! Two seconds and a first, right?"

Lani shrugged. "Guess they figure there's still room for improvement."

Dylan was squinting at someone over Malory's left shoulder. "Hey, is that Clare over there? What's with her?"

The group turned and searched for where Dylan was pointing in the crowd.

"Well," Lani began, "I'm guessing she's going on more about how this afternoon's performance marks the first sign of the apocalypse for Chestnut Hill."

"I was in the buffet line next to her," Malory said, "and she was going on about how Sara should be mad at Ms. Carmichael for Mischief Maker's injury. It sounds like it's a stone bruise, so he probably landed wrong on something that was in the ring."

"But that's not necessarily Ali's fault," Dylan said, her hands finding their way to her hips. "She had the arena dragged twice over break. He could have stepped on something that fell out of another horse's hoof."

"I know," Malory agreed in a slightly defensive tone. "You try telling Clare that."

If Dylan had been feeling better, she might have marched over to Clare and cleared everything right up, but she couldn't exactly think straight with her head in a haze. Besides, she had just spotted Caleb striding toward them with a couple of his St. Kits teammates.

"Aha!" Dylan greeted him with a grin. "Here he is, the man of the hour — the best junior rider in the All Schools League."

Caleb gave a mock bow. "Thank you, thank you!" he said playfully.

He introduced the girls to his teammates, Eddie and Philip. "There's some good grub at this party," said Eddie, a wiry boy with a shock of outrageously red hair and a plate piled high with finger food. "You Chestnut Hillers have a good sense of hospitality."

"Your riding's not too bad, either," Philip added. He was taller than either Eddie or Caleb, with dark hair and a serious but friendly expression. "You guys both had good rounds. The other riders had some bad luck, but you'll give us a run for our money next time."

"We'll still win though, of course," Caleb added.

Malory punched him playfully on the arm. "We'll see," she said, her blue eyes sparkling. "Just wait until we get our cross-country course constructed, you'll be whimpering in awe then."

Dylan was glad to see that Malory was finally getting comfortable enough about her friendship with Caleb to tease him back. She only wished she could get rid of the throbbing pulse beating behind her eyes so she could enjoy the banter more. "Stupid headache," she muttered.

"What was that?" Philip asked, glancing over at her.

"Nothing." Dylan forced a smile, deciding that her ailment was a case of mind over matter. All she had to do was distract herself, and she would be fine. "So you're the one with that cool Appaloosa Sport Horse, right?" she asked Philip.

"Yeah. He's an App–Thoroughbred cross," Philip replied. "His show name's Spots of Fun."

Dylan laughed. "Good one. He definitely looks spots of fun to ride. . . ." she rolled her eyes at her own weak joke, realizing her headache was now compounded by other symptoms—a decidedly lame sense of humor for starters.

She spent the next few minutes chatting with Philip and Eddie. They were very curious about the plans for the cross-country course, and, even though Dylan was psyched for the new addition to the riding program, she didn't feel like her explanation was coherent. Then somebody lowered the lights and turned on the sound system, and the dancing started. Normally there was nothing Dylan loved more than a party. But as her headache battled to take over, she had to work harder and harder to stay focused on having fun. It felt exhausting just standing there talking to people, let alone dancing. Within minutes, her throat started to hurt from shouting to be heard over the pulsing music.

"Listen, I think I'm going to bail," she told Lani, who was bopping to the hip-hop song blasting out of the speakers.

Lani looked surprised. "But it's only seven thirty!"

Dylan shrugged. "I know," she said. "I guess I wore myself out today. Tell Caleb and everyone I said goodbye, okay?" Without waiting for an answer, she turned and hurried away, suddenly so exhausted she wasn't sure she was going to make it across the campus and up the stairs to her room.

The next morning Dylan awoke with chills, a stuffed-up nose, and a queasy stomach. "Ugh," she rasped as Honey gazed down at her with a worried look on her pretty heart-shaped face, "I thought I was just tired and headachy from the show yesterday. Guess it was more than that."

"Stay put — I'll go get Ms. Herson," Honey said.

"No, I'll be okay." Dylan struggled to push herself into an upright position. "I just need a little breakfast to settle my stomach and clear my head."

"Forget it." Honey's voice was firm. She pulled her bathrobe shut and tied it around her waist. "I'm fetching Hersie right now." She hurried out of the room without giving Dylan a chance to protest further.

Dylan sank back against her pillow. She tried to close her mouth, but soon found it impossible to breathe that way. She wished she had a tissue, but it seemed like far too much effort to get up and walk over to her dresser in search of one.

Just then Lynsey wandered back into the room from the bathroom. Even though it was Sunday, she was already fully dressed in her favorite skinny-leg True Religion jeans and a green L.A.M.B. hoodie. "What's with you?" she asked Dylan, wrinkling her nose. "You look terrible."

"Gee, thanks." Dylan paused to cough. "Same to you."

"Ew!" Lynsey took a step backward, as if fearing Dylan's next cough might spew phlegm all over her outfit. "I'm out of here. Try not to sneeze on my bed while I'm gone, okay?"

She swept out of the room, and Dylan leaned back and closed her eyes. The next thing she knew, she was looking up at the concerned face of Ms. Herson, Adams dorm's middle school housemother.

"You're right, Honey," Ms. Herson said, putting the back of her hand to Dylan's forehead. "She definitely needs to stay in bed. Try to get back to sleep, Dylan. I'll stop by after breakfast to check on you."

Dylan tried to argue, but found herself too exhausted. So she gave in and slipped back into a dream-soaked slumber, hardly aware of Honey and Ms. Herson leaving the room.

She woke up abruptly some time later, feeling a little more alert. Glancing at the clock radio on her bedside table, she saw that it was well after lunchtime.

Hearing a thump from across the room, she realized she must have been awakened by Lynsey's entrance. Her roommate was rummaging through her wardrobe over near the window.

Hearing Dylan cough, she turned around. "Oh," Lynsey said. "You're awake. Are you still sick?"

"No. I'm practicing my Method acting for my next starring film role," Dylan said hoarsely, stifling another cough. "I'm playing a victim of the bubonic plague. Do you think I'll get the part?"

Lynsey rolled her eyes. "Lame jokes, bad hair — yeah, I'd say you're just about back to normal. If you can call anything about you *normal*."

Dylan was trying to figure out if she could projectile-sneeze all the way across the room to where Lynsey was standing when Honey, Lani, and Malory came into the room. "Dylan!" Lani cried. "You're alive! Awake, even!"

Dylan grinned, already feeling a little better. "You bet," she said. "So what'd I miss while I was passed out?"

"Not much." Honey sat down on the edge of her bed. "We just came from the stable."

"And don't worry," Malory added. "We made sure to make a big fuss over Morello for you."

"Good." Dylan sneezed into a tissue, then leaned back against her pillow. "So how are all the horses today? How's Mischief Maker?"

"Still lame," Malory said. "Sara's keeping him on stall rest with an Easyboot just to be safe. She's terrified that he's going to get an abscess and be off for the rest of the school year. But, if the recovery goes well, he might just be out a show or two."

"Phew!" Dylan exclaimed. "I really didn't want to think about our chances for the All Schools Trophy without Sara and Mischief on the team."

Lani grimaced. "After yesterday's show, we're all terrified about that. Even Ms. Carmichael was muttering something about pushing us harder in riding class from now on."

"Never mind that," Honey said. "How are you doing, Dylan? Feeling any better?"

"I hate being sick," Dylan said with a frown. "I really hate it. I always feel like I'm missing all sorts of interesting stuff while I'm stuck in bed all miserable and sniffly and stuff."

Malory smiled sympathetically. "When I get the flu, my dad always brings me a little bell that I can use to summon him from the store. It's like having my own personal servant."

Lynsey let out an audible snort. "Excuse me," she said, pushing her way between Lani and Malory. "Maybe you people enjoy hanging around this makeshift sickroom, but I have better things to do."

"Like visiting Bluegrass and giving him a nice grooming after yesterday's effort, maybe?" Lani said pointedly. "Kelly said she hadn't seen you all day."

"Thanks, Mom," Lynsey retorted. Without another word, she swept off into the hall.

Dylan wasn't sorry to see her go. "Okay, back to this bell thing," she said. "I'm liking this idea. If you guys get me one, I can keep you apprised of the schedule: I'm thinking we should have cookies and soda at two, a gossip gabfest at two thirty, followed by a foot massage from Malory at three." She stuck one bare foot out from under the covers and waggled her toes hopefully.

Lani wrinkled her nose. "Cookies and soda, maybe," she said. "Touching your stanky ol' bare feet? No way."

"Besides, we don't have a bell." Malory snapped her fingers. "Too bad!"

Dylan held up her hand, crooking her thumb and

index finger as if holding the handle of a tiny bell. "Ding-a-ling-a-ling!" she croaked. "Time to fetch the patient some Cool Ranch Doritos!"

"Is that really what she should be eating?" Honey inquired.

"Oh, what the heck." Lani headed for the door. "I'll see what they've got in the vending machine. . . ."

Lani returned a few minutes later with several small bags of potato chips and other snacks. The four girls spent the next half hour eating and hanging out. But Dylan hardly touched the food. Still, Dylan thought that even without the bell, the afternoon had pretty much gone as planned — minus the massage.

By the time Ms. Herson turned up to check on Dylan and shooed the others out, Dylan was in a better mood, but she was also completely exhausted.

"You've still got a bit of a fever," Ms. Herson said, feeling her forehead.

"My mom would say I just need a good night's sleep," Dylan murmured, already wishing to be alone. All she could think about was closing her eyes and leaning her aching head on her cool, soft pillow. "I'm sure I'll be all better by tomorrow. . . ."

CHAPTER FIVE

On Monday morning Dylan awoke feeling as if her head was stuffed with cotton and her throat had been rubbed with sandpaper. For a moment she thought she was also suffering from a strange buzzing in her ears, but she soon realized it was only Lynsey's alarm clock. Her roommate had gone into the bathroom without bothering to turn it off.

In her bed near the door, Honey sat up and rubbed her eyes. "What time is it?" she mumbled.

"Uuurgh," was the only response Dylan could muster.

That seemed to bring Honey to full consciousness. She looked over at Dylan, who was still lying flat on her back staring at the ceiling. "How are you feeling? Any better?"

Dylan blinked. That took so much effort that she wasn't sure she would be able to respond to Honey's question. "Off," she croaked at last, lifting one hand long enough to wave toward Lynsey's bed before her hand flopped back onto her sheets.

Honey pushed her blonde hair out of her eyes, then hopped out of bed and hurried across the room to turn off the offending alarm. Once the room was quiet again, she walked over and stared down at Dylan.

"You don't look so good," she said. "I think I'd better call Ms. Herson again."

A half hour later, Dylan was staring up at the blue-painted ceiling of the large room fondly known as the Sick Suite. Located on the first floor of Adams dorm near Ms. Herson's living quarters, it was where the housemothers put students who were too sick to attend class. When a virus was going around campus, there might be as many as a half dozen girls staying there in single beds divided by folding screens. But Dylan was the only one there that particular day, and so the screens were stacked against the wall, leaving the entire room open to her view and leaving her feeling intensely alone without her friends.

"I could've stayed in my own room," Dylan mumbled as Ms. Herson bustled around, pulling down the window shade and fluffing the quilt.

"Nonsense," the housemother said. "You don't want your roommates catching this, do you?"

Dylan had to stop and think about that. Naturally

there was no way she would ever wish her present misery on Honey. Lynsey, on the other hand . . . She was still pondering the delicious possibilities as she drifted off to sleep.

☙

"Surprise!"

Dylan was watching a documentary about wheat farming on the Sick Suite's TV when her three best friends burst in later that afternoon. She immediately grabbed the remote and switched off the TV.

"Get in here — I need a social infusion!" she cried hoarsely.

Malory leaned against the dresser. "How was your day?"

"This room doesn't have cable. Need I say more? What did I miss in the real world?"

Lani perched at the far end of the bed. "Mme. Dubois missed you in French class. There wasn't anyone for her to chastise," she teased. "And when we told Dr. Duffy you were sick, he looked like he didn't believe us. You know you missed the botany exam, right."

Dylan rolled her eyes. French and science were her two least favorite classes. "Okay, maybe there are some advantages to being sick. I could use the extra time to study — and maybe some pointers from someone who most likely aced it," she said, looking pointedly at Lani, who was a star pupil in math and science. Dylan paused to cough. "How was riding class today?"

"Great!" Honey said, her whole face lighting up. "Ms. Carmichael said she wants me to try riding Minnie!"

"Isn't that great?" Lani exclaimed. "Ms. C. suggested Honey come in for a private lesson on Saturday."

Malory nodded. "That will be a good way to start Minuet off easy," she said.

"That's so cool, Honey," Dylan said. "You must be so psyched. It's about time!"

"I am," Honey admitted. "I'm a bit nervous, though."

"Don't be," Dylan assured her. "You'll do great. Minnie adores you. Plus, you're a much better rider than Patience — even without stirrups. So what else happened?"

"Ms. Carmichael had us try a new jumping exercise," Lani said. "It was kind of weird. She set up this double line of little jumps, and we had to do it in pairs and try to stay right with each other the whole way through."

"Fun!" Dylan's heart sank at the discovery that she'd missed a new and interesting exercise. "How'd everybody do?"

"Lani had to pair up with Lynsey." Honey laughed. "You should have seen Lynsey's face — she didn't think any of the other ponies were good enough to pair up with Bluegrass. Especially not a pony with a *Western* pedigree."

Dylan grimaced, twisting the bedsheet between her hands. "Sounds like Lynsey."

"Yeah, but Colorado and I showed her." Lani's eyes sparkled. "We stayed right with Blue just like we were supposed to — even when he broke stride right after the second jump. I bet Lynsey did that just to try to mess us up!"

"That sounds like her. Leave it to her to mess up Blue just to try to make you look bad. That girl is totally diabolical."

"Yeah, it was interesting," Lani agreed. "Ms. C. didn't correct anyone for any mistakes, just if they didn't stay with their partner."

Dylan glanced at Malory, who hadn't said anything about the exercise yet. "How'd Tybalt do?"

Malory shrugged. "As well as can be expected," she said. "I wasn't sure he was ready for something like that, but Ms. Carmichael really wanted us to try it. He got a little fast and excited when he saw the other pony next to him."

"But you handled him great," Lani assured her. "You should've seen her, Dyl — Tybalt let out this little buck at the end, and Mal stayed superglued to the saddle!"

They chatted about other barn gossip and school news for a few more minutes. But far too soon, Dylan felt her energy flagging. As her friends described something particularly stupid Patience had said in math class, she stifled a yawn.

Malory looked at her with concern. "Maybe we'd better let you rest."

"No!" Dylan protested, though a coughing spell prevented her saying anything else.

Lani checked her watch. "Actually, we do have to go," she said. "It's taco night at the dining hall, and if we don't get there early, all the guacamole will be gone."

Honey patted Dylan's knee through the bedcovers. "We'll come see you again tomorrow," she said. "Make sure you get lots of sleep. I want you better in time to come watch me ride Minnie on Saturday."

"I'll be there, even if they have to bring me on a stretcher," Dylan promised. Even though she wished her friends could stay longer, she didn't really mind too much when they hurried off. Getting some sleep suddenly seemed like an awfully appealing idea.

❧

Dylan awakened from her nap at around seven P.M. Her head was still fuzzy and echoey from the flu but her stomach felt a little better, so she ate the crackers Ms. Herson had left her and drank a glass and a half of water from the carafe by her bed. Then she grabbed her BlackBerry from the bedside table to check her e-mail. There was one from her parents, several from friends back home in Connecticut, and one from Henri, a French boy she'd met on a ski trip over the holiday break. Dylan's heart pounded as she opened up Henri's message.

Bonjour, Dylan, he wrote. *Got your e-mail. Sorry to hear you are sick. I hope you are feeling better soon. Your friend, Henri.*

Dylan shrugged. It wasn't the longest or most romantic message in the world. But then again, Henri's English was shaky at best. Given Dylan's French, it wasn't like she would be writing Henri sonnets in his language, either.

When she heard the door open, she glanced up, expecting to see Ms. Herson or Nurse O'Connor. Instead, she saw Ali Carmichael coming in with an armful of magazines.

"Knock knock," Ali said with a smile. "Anybody home?"

"Hey!" Dylan greeted her, tossing aside her BlackBerry and sitting up. "What are you doing here?"

"What do you think?" her aunt teased. "I came to drag you down to the barn to muck out stalls."

Dylan let out a mock groan, putting one hand to her head. "Bad news," she said. "Nurse O'Connor said I'm so deathly ill that I won't be able to do any barn chores for the rest of the year. Oh, but lots of riding is extremely important to my recovery. . . ."

"Very funny," Ali said with a laugh. "I may have to check in with her about that diagnosis." She stepped forward and set her magazines on the table. "In the meantime, I thought you might want to look through these while you're stuck in bed. They're old copies of *Practical Horseman.*"

"Cool, thanks!" Dylan leaned over to get a better look at the magazine pile, glad that her aunt had stopped by. The two of them had gotten a lot closer since spending spring break together. It was nice to have the chance to slip back into that more relaxed relationship for a little while instead of having to act the part of teacher and student. "So how are things at the barn?" she asked. "Is everyone still bumming about the show?"

Ali frowned slightly. "Not that I've noticed," she said. "As a matter of fact, I'm not convinced anyone is really spending any time thinking about why we lost."

"Oh." Dylan wasn't sure how to respond to that. Was it her fever, or did Ali sound kind of annoyed? But at the moment, phlegmy and tired as she was, it seemed like way too much effort to figure it out.

Dylan had found a copy of the most recent *Teen People* cleverly slipped in between the horse magazines Ali had dropped off, and she was paging through it the next afternoon when Honey and Lani came by to visit again. When they entered, Dylan wanted to jump up and hug them despite her germs. She felt as if she'd been in limbo all day — too sick to go back to her regular life, but just better enough to feel restless and bored by spending another day in bed.

"Thank God you're here!" she cried dramatically. "It's like I'm serving solitary confinement! It's cruel and unusual punishment, making me stare at these pastel walls all day!"

"She's sounding more like her usual self today," Honey remarked to Lani.

"Yeah. Too bad, huh?" Lani replied. She grinned and ducked as Dylan winged her magazine at her head. "I can tell you're still weak. That was a pathetic throw."

"Very funny." Dylan pretended to pout as Lani retrieved the magazine and tossed it back to her. "It's not nice to tease a sick person, you know." She glanced at the empty doorway behind them. "So where's Mal? Doesn't she care enough to come visit her poor bedridden friend today?"

"She said to tell you she'll stop in later," Honey reported. "She's still down at the barn showing Sara some T-touch stuff to use on Mischief."

Dylan nodded. Malory had learned a lot from books and magazines on alternative methods of taking care of horses, and even more from the Web site of the nearby Heartland horse sanctuary and Heartland's owner, Amy Fleming. One of her favorite techniques was T-touch, a system developed by Linda Tellington-Jones to help horses by using specialized massage movements.

"Cool," she said. "I bet Mischief will love that. So what else is new?"

"Well, you missed a big throw-down at the barn just now." Lani grimaced. "It was pretty grizzly. Clare Houlder was mouthing off to Ms. Carmichael during the advanced lesson."

"Really?" With a tremor of alarm, Dylan recalled Clare's bad-tempered rant at the show on Saturday. "What did she say?"

Lani's brown eyes took on the sharp gleam they always got when she was angry or annoyed. "Nothing that made much sense," she replied. "She was having trouble with this tough new jumping grid Ms. Carmichael had set up — Sancha kept rushing and messing up the striding — and then Clare freaked out! She yanked Sancha to a stop and started whining about how Ms. Mitchell never made them do tricky combinations like that, she never had any trouble jumping anything on Snapdragon, blah, blah, blah."

Dylan gasped so loudly that it set off a coughing fit. It was true that Ali liked to train with grids — tight sequences of fences that required absolute precision from horse and rider — more than the average riding instructor. Grids weren't as much fun as courses, but she was still surprised Clare lashed out like that. "No way!" she said when she could speak again.

"Way," Lani confirmed. "It was ugly."

"Ms. Carmichael didn't let things get too out of hand, though," Honey said. "She just made Clare sit there and watch while the others did it, then at the end she had her give comments on the others' rides."

"It would take more than crazy Clare to rattle her," Lani said. "After all, she has to handle Princess Lynsey's antics on a daily basis. If she can do that without losing her temper, this was nothing!"

Honey laughed. "Too true!" she agreed. "Anyway, I'm sure Clare was just frustrated because she was messing up in front of everyone. We all know how defensive she gets."

"Yeah, she's got some issues," Dylan said. "But does anyone else think she's been even worse than usual lately? At the show the other day she and the other C's kept complaining about everything — especially Aunt Ali. And now this . . ."

Lani shrugged. "I wouldn't worry about it," she said. "Nobody pays much attention to those three anyway."

"I guess." Dylan leaned back against her pillow as a wave of exhaustion swept over her. Her friends continued to chat, but she found her mind wandering. Her flu might be making her paranoid, but she couldn't shake the feeling that Clare and her friends were doing more than complaining about Aunt Ali.

CHAPTER SIX

By Wednesday morning Dylan was starting to feel less like a wet dishrag and more like herself. When Ms. Herson took her temperature, it was almost back to normal.

"Does that mean I can move back to my own room?" Dylan asked.

"Hmm." The housemother examined the mercury in her thermometer. "Let's give it another half day, just in case. I don't want you starting an outbreak."

With some effort, Dylan managed not to roll her eyes. "I'm sure I'm not contagious anymore," she said. "And I'm going totally nuts being stuck here. Can I at least go for a walk?"

"Well . . ."

Dylan pasted a pleading expression on her face and waited. "All right," the housemother relented at last. "I suppose that would be all right. But keep it short."

"I promise!" Not giving her a chance to change her

mind, Dylan hopped out of bed and reached for the clothes Honey had brought downstairs for her the previous day.

Outside, she paused just long enough to take a few big gulps of the crisp, clean winter air. Then she turned and made a beeline for the stable. Her limbs felt weak and shaky after three full days in bed, but she found herself walking faster the closer she got to the barn doors.

"Ah, that wonderful smell of manure!" she cried out as the first whiff of horsey scent reached her on a passing breeze. She spread her arms wide as if to embrace the entire stable area. "Gotta love it!"

A passing ninth-grader whose name she couldn't remember gave her a dubious look, but Dylan ignored it. She had just spotted several horses filing into the outdoor jumping ring with riders up. Hurrying closer, she realized a sophomore advanced lesson was about to begin.

Chestnut Hill's part-time jumping coach, Alden Phillips, was just closing the gate behind the last rider when Dylan reached the ring. The trainer shot her a surprised look. "Shouldn't you be in class?"

"I just escaped from my sickroom," Dylan explained. "I've had the flu since Sunday, so now I'm out for a few minutes getting some fresh air and exercise — you know, kind of like a horse coming back from a layup." She grinned, pleased with her simile. "Mind if I watch for a while?"

"Be my guest." Ms. Phillips smiled at her, then strode out toward the center of the ring. "All right, class!" she called to the girls warming up their horses and ponies along the rail. "I'll give you a few moments to get the kinks out. Meanwhile I'll be setting up a couple of grids for us to work through today."

"Grids?" Jessica Jones called back, sounding surprised. "I thought we were supposed to be doing courses today."

Dylan rolled her eyes. She loved the special challenge of grids, but some of the other riders seemed to think that any jumping lesson that didn't involve full courses like the ones they rode in shows was a waste of time.

"Change of plan," the coach said. "Ms. Carmichael wants us to focus on adjustability today, and these particular grids should help with that. We're also supposed to try something new — after each ride, we're going to have a group critique. Each of you is going to come up with one piece of constructive criticism for the rider and one compliment. That way we can all learn from one another."

"What?" Sophie Chatterton wrinkled her nose. "That sounds kind of weird." As the coach shot her a stern look, Sophie smiled contritely. "Um, I mean, it sounds like all that critiquing is going to take up an awful lot of time."

Ms. Phillips shrugged. "I guess we'll find out," she

said. "If there's time at the end and everyone is doing well, we may throw in a course or two."

Dylan leaned on the fence. She always found it educational to watch the more experienced riders' lessons. Even though the girls in this class were only three years older, some of them already had a lifetime of experience. Jessica's father was a racing trainer in New York, Natasha Appleby was a rising star in the Big Eq classes out in her home state of California, and Jillian Watt and Sophie Chatterton competed all summer on the East Coast A circuit.

After warming up on the flat, the riders started taking the grids one by one. Nobody had any trouble with the first exercise, even when Ms. Phillips raised the heights. Dylan noticed that after the first couple of rides, the coach stopped insisting on individual critiques.

Then the class moved on to the second set of jumps. Jillian and Natasha rode through easily, but Helen Sullivan, who was riding Lani's favorite pony Colorado, got off stride and wound up crashing through the last element. Colorado was nervous and quick the second time through, though they managed not to knock anything down that round. After that, everyone seemed to start riding more cautiously, which caused a few problems. It took several more times through to get everyone comfortable with the gymnastic, and by the time they moved on to the third grid, the class was almost over, leaving no time for coursework — or critiques — after all.

As the lesson ended, Dylan was itching to get back in the saddle herself. "Nice riding, guys," she said as the sophomores rode past her out of the ring. "I wish I was allowed to try those grids," she added, realizing how pathetic she sounded.

Jessica let out a snort. "Be careful what you wish for," she muttered.

Dylan shrugged and trailed into the barn after the older girls, planning to spend a few minutes with Morello before returning to the Sick Suite. As she rounded the corner into the main stable aisle, she had to stop short. She almost ran right into Lucky's rear end. His rider, Jillian Watt, had stopped him there and was talking to Sophie Chatterton as she slipped Lucky's bridle off.

". . . and then Ms. C. doesn't even want us doing courses the very next week!" Jillian was saying. "It doesn't make sense. Liz Mitchell would've had us practicing over the same course we messed up on until we could do it in our sleep!"

"I hear you," Sophie replied as she wiped the sweat off Gandalf's face with a rag. "How are we supposed to compete against those other schools if we . . ."

She suddenly glanced over and spotted Dylan standing there. Immediately, she stopped what she was saying and pasted a sickly sweet smile on her face.

Jillian turned and saw her, too. "Oh, hi," she said lamely. "Sorry, do you need to get by?" Clicking to Lucky, she moved him on toward the wash stall.

Dylan stood where she was for a moment. She was already worried that the three C's had turned against Ali. And now, with Clare and her friends nowhere in sight, other competent riders were starting to sound just like them! Exactly what had she missed during those three days while she was sick in bed?

"Hey, Dylan." Her aunt's voice interrupted her thoughts. "Does your housemother know you're out of bed?"

Dylan spun around to face Ali. She didn't want to worry her with what she'd just overheard — not until she was sure it was something to worry about.

"Yeah, she said I could go for a walk," Dylan said. "So I figured, what better place to walk to than here?"

Ali gave a knowing smile. "Fine. But don't wear yourself out, okay?" She turned toward the others. "How did today's lesson go?" she called out.

"Those grids were hard," Natasha said.

"They were meant to be," Ali replied. "As I told you on Monday, we're going to be stepping up the challenge level from here on out. Did the individual critiques help you figure out how to ride the grids better?"

The sophomores traded slightly guilty glances. "Um, sort of," Jessica said. "I mean, not everyone had something to say. And we didn't really have time to do that after *every* ride. But it was interesting the first couple of times."

Ali frowned. "But that was the whole point . . ." Her voice trailed off and she shook her head. "Where's Coach Phillips?"

Dylan watched her aunt stomp off down the aisle. "What was that all about?" she muttered to Morello, who was sticking his head out of his stall nearby. She had never seen her aunt react that way. *I spend a few days out with the flu, and when I get back everyone is acting weird.*

🐎

"Are you sure you feel okay enough to eat this glop?" Lani lifted her fork, allowing the bean-and-vegetable casserole to plop back down onto her plate.

"I've barely eaten a thing for the past three and a half days, remember?" Dylan scooped up a big bite of her dinner. "To me, this glop is heaven!"

She might have been exaggerating a little bit about the casserole, but she *was* thrilled that Ms. Herson and Nurse O'Connor had finally released her from the Sick Suite. Her friends had helped her move back upstairs after classes, and now they were all having dinner together in the cafeteria.

"Want to go down and visit the barn after we eat?" Malory asked her. "You must be missing Morello like crazy."

Dylan swallowed her food. "I stopped in to see him today, but I didn't get to stay long." She hesitated, glancing around to make sure nobody at the neighboring tables was paying attention to their conversation. "I kind of wanted to get out of there. People were giving me the willies."

"What do you mean?" Honey asked, poking suspiciously at a lump in her serving of casserole.

"The sophomores were riding," Dylan said. "And when they were done, they were complaining. A lot."

Lani rolled her eyes. "Stop the presses!" she joked as she speared a chunk of carrot with her fork. "Let me guess — they were griping about not having private grooms to help them untack like they do on the circuit."

"Not quite," Dylan said. "Everyone was being super-dramatic, talking about Ali. It reminded me of some stuff the Three C's were saying at the show. Asking why they weren't practicing courses. And comparing Ali to Liz Mitchell."

Malory shrugged. "So what? Clare's always whining about something. It's probably more of her griping about not being picked for the senior team this year."

"That's what I thought, too," Dylan said. "Especially after what you guys told me about how she flipped out in her riding class. But the snarkiness seemed weird coming from Sophie and Jillian. And then, Ali got all upset about how Coach Phillips didn't have everyone critique each other. It was all very odd."

"Maybe it's a full moon or something," Lani suggested. "That would explain why everyone's wigging out."

Honey looked more sympathetic. "I don't blame you for worrying a little," she told Dylan. "But you're probably just extra sensitive. You know, because Ali's your aunt."

"And because you've been sick," Malory put in, reaching for her water glass. "I know I always feel all emotional and weird when I have the flu."

I'm not all emotional, Dylan thought with a flash of resentment. *And it's not just because she's my aunt. I know what I heard. . . .*

But she quickly shook off the indignant feeling. The last thing she wanted to do was pick an argument with her friends on her first night back in the real world. She would just have to keep her ear to the ground and figure out herself if there really was something going on.

🐎

"Malory! Wait up!"

Dylan and her friends stopped short as they entered the dorm lobby. Dinner had just ended, and they were hurrying to reach the lounge in time to watch a movie with their friends Razina Jackson, Alexandra Cooper, and Wei Lin Chang.

Turning to see who had called Malory's name, Dylan

blinked. "What's Lynsey want with you?" she asked her friend.

"You got me." Malory looked as surprised as Dylan felt. Lynsey had to interact quite a bit with Dylan and Honey, since they were her roommates. And Lani pretty much forced everyone around to interact with her due to her fearless, outspoken personality. Out of the four of them, Malory was probably the one least likely to speak to with Lynsey on any given day. And unless Lynsey was growling at her to get out of her way during riding class, it was generally mutual.

Lynsey hurried toward them. She had changed out of her school uniform for dinner and was dressed in what Dylan was pretty sure was a head-to-toe Stella McCartney for Adidas tracksuit. Really, could Lynsey not dress herself if she didn't match up all of the labels?

"I need to talk to you," she said, stopping in front of Malory and tossing her long blonde hair over her shoulder.

"Um, about what?" Malory asked.

Lynsey shot a suspicious glance at the other girls. "It's private," she told Malory. "We can go up to my room and talk there."

Dylan narrowed her eyes. "Mysterious much?" she commented.

Lynsey ignored her. "Come on, Malory." She slung her Jana Feifer bag over her shoulder and grabbed Malory's arm. With a confused shrug at her friends, Malory allowed herself to be dragged off toward the lobby's ornate double staircase.

"That was weird," Lani said as she watched the odd couple hurry up the steps and disappear on the landing above.

"Weird is an understatement." Dylan took a step in the direction the pair had disappeared, wishing she could be a fly on the wall. "Since when does Lynsey even notice that Mal exists?"

Lani shrugged. "Who knows? Anyway, I'm sure Mal will tell us what it's about when she's done."

Lani was right, of course. But Dylan didn't have that kind of patience. "I'll meet you guys in the lounge in a few minutes," she said. "I have to stop by the room to — to — um, change my shoes."

Honey and Lani looked skeptical, but Dylan didn't give them enough time to respond. Spinning on her heel, she raced off toward the stairs.

Rushing across the landing and up the second stairway two steps at a time, she soon found herself standing outside the door of Room Two. The door was ajar, and she paused there and held her breath, trying to hear what was going on inside. But all she could hear was the soft murmur of voices — she couldn't make out what they were saying.

She pushed the door open farther, trying to stay quiet.

But Lynsey and Malory immediately stopped talking and turned to look at her. Lynsey was standing between her bed and her desk, while Malory sat perched on the edge of the desk chair.

"Don't mind me," Dylan sang out innocently, strolling into the room. "I just came up to get something."

Lynsey crossed her arms. "Well, get it and get out. We're trying to have a private conversation here."

"You can't tell me to get out," Dylan countered. "This is my room, too."

"Fine." Lynsey scowled at her, then gestured to Malory. "Come on. We'll go somewhere else to talk."

Malory didn't say a word, though she did shoot Dylan an apologetic smile as she followed Lynsey out of the room. Dylan slumped on the edge of Honey's bed, wondering if she should try to follow them.

Lani found her there a few minutes later. "Find those shoes?" she asked.

"Huh?" Dylan smiled sheepishly, glancing down at her feet. "Um, I guess I changed my mind about that."

"Mal and Lynsey got away from you, huh?"

"Yeah," Dylan admitted with a sigh, trying to fight back her own curiosity. "Lynsey might be annoying, but she's not stupid. I figured there's no point in trying to follow them."

Lani smiled. "Good. Then come on — the movie's about to start."

🐎

"I can't believe I'm not allowed to ride for almost a week," Dylan grumbled as she watched her friends tack up for their riding class the next day. Lani had Colorado in cross-ties outside his stall, while Honey tacked up a dark bay pony named Falcon in the next set of ties down the aisle. Malory was tacking Tybalt in his stall, as usual, since the gelding seemed to prefer it that way. The other members of their class were all either at the other barn or in their ponies' stalls.

Lani shot Dylan a sympathetic look as she tightened Colorado's girth. "I know how you feel," she said. "When I hurt my wrist, I was off for two whole weeks, remember? At least you're allowed to watch." She slipped Colorado's bridle over his nose. "You're lucky it's not colder out, or they'd probably make you sit in study hall at the library or something."

Dylan had to admit she had a point. But it didn't make her feel much better. Neither did the fact that Malory still hadn't told anyone what Lynsey had wanted with her the evening before. She'd turned up halfway through the movie saying it was no big deal, but she couldn't talk about it. No matter how hard Dylan had tried, she couldn't get any more than that out of her. Dylan knew that her friend could be private, but this was ridiculous!

She trailed along as the others led their ponies to the

outdoor dressage arena. Today was scheduled to be a flat class, and they found Roger Musgrave, the part-time equitation coach, waiting for them with his watch in hand.

"You're late!" he barked out in his crisp English accent as Malory and Honey took turns using the mounting block outside the gate. Lani bypassed the block, swinging on from the ground. Lynsey and her friend Nadia Simon were already waiting on their ponies in the ring, along with Heidi Johnson and Paris Mackenzie. "We have a lot to cover today — you! Miss Walsh. Why are you still on foot?"

Dylan explained what Ali and Ms. Herson had decreed. "But hey, if you want to overrule them . . ." she started hopefully.

In response, Mr. Musgrave pointed sternly with his crop toward the small set of bleachers outside the ring. But Dylan swore she spotted a twinkle in his eye as he turned away to check the others' tack.

She spent every minute of the next forty wishing she could be in the ring with the others. She was so busy watching Nadia trying to get her pony Hardy to do a proper shoulder-in that she didn't notice Ali striding across the stable yard until she was passing right in front of her.

"Hey," Dylan called to her aunt, quickly sliding down to the lowest bleacher. "Did you come to tell me I can ride in the next lesson?"

"What?" Ali stopped short and stared at her, not really seeming to see her for a second. "Oh! Dylan. No, nothing like that. I was just on my way to the office."

"What's wrong?" Dylan forgot about her own problems for a moment as she noticed her aunt's harried expression.

Ali sighed. "I just got off the phone with the construction company that's building our cross-country course. Apparently there's some kind of emergency with the two-star course over at the state park — damage from that ice storm last month, I think — and the construction company needs to drop everything and take care of that before getting back to us. Looks like our project will probably be delayed about a month."

"No way!" Dylan exclaimed. "That stinks."

"I know." Ali shrugged. "But the park's first three-day event of the season is scheduled for the first week in April, which means they're going to have to take priority."

"Oh, well." Dylan tried to hide her disappointment, knowing it wasn't Ali's fault. "No big deal. I'm sure everyone will understand."

"I know that's probably true," Ali responded, still looking anxious. "But it's never easy to be the bearer of bad news. The school was really hoping to have the course finished on schedule." With that, Ali continued on her trek to the office.

Dylan looked after her as she walked away. She

considered what her aunt said and a feeling of uneasiness swept over her.

But by the time Dylan and her friends stopped by the barn after dinner that evening, they found the place buzzing with the bad news about the cross-country course.

"It's really too bad," Anita Demarco was saying as they walked in. "It would have been a great draw to prospective students to have a professionally constructed cross-country course here on campus."

"Not to mention that the graduating seniors might never get to try it if it's delayed much more," added Sara Chappell, who was soaking Mischief Maker's injured foot in the wash stall.

"I'd say the eventing course is the least of our worries." Natasha Appleby was pulling the mane of a horse named Highland Fling in the cross-ties nearby. "Our biggest draw for prospective students — at least the ones who ride — used to be our winning jumping teams." She shifted her pulling comb to her other hand. "Now we don't even have that anymore."

"Yeah, it's kind of depressing." Anita grimaced. "My mother has a couple of friends who went to Allbright's, and she said they were totally razzing her about last weekend's show."

As she listened to the older girls, Dylan's stomach started to churn. And this time it had nothing to do with the flu.

"Did you hear that?" she whispered to her friends when they'd moved past the older girls. "The upperclassmen sound really upset about this cross-country course delay. And now it sounds like they're ready to blame Aunt Ali for everything from our loss at the show to the national debt. . . ."

"Are you still on that?" Malory glanced at her. "I thought we convinced you it was all in your head."

"Yeah." Lani shrugged. "I mean, they might be a little down on Ms. Carmichael since she's been pushing us all pretty hard this week. But it'll blow over — no big deal."

Dylan didn't bother to respond. She stared back down the aisle, a worried crease in her forehead. It was one thing for cranky Clare and her pals to gripe about Ali, or even for some of the more gossipy types like Patience or Lynsey to take their cue from the older girls. But now it sounded as if even the more levelheaded upperclassmen like Sara and Anita were picking up on the anti-Ali sentiment.

Maybe her friends couldn't see it yet, but there was no longer any doubt in Dylan's mind. This was mutiny!

CHAPTER SEVEN

The next day was Friday, and the day dawned unseasonably warm and sunny, giving a hint of the coming change of seasons. With the Spring Fling dance being held at St. Kits in eight days and counting, shopping for party outfits was rapidly becoming a priority. Students weren't allowed to leave campus during the week except with special permission, but on Saturdays there was a bus service from the school to nearby Cheney Falls. The small town didn't have anything approaching the kind of shopping available in New York City, which was just a train ride away from Dylan's home in Connecticut. But there was a shopping mall at one end of town, along with a flea market and a small but flourishing business district that featured a mix of restaurants, antique stores, and interesting boutiques. With their last chance to go to town a day away, the girls were busy finalizing outfits and shopping plans.

"... and so I told Razina she could borrow that turquoise necklace I ... Dylan? Did you hear a word I just said?"

"Huh?" Dylan blinked and looked up at Lani, who was glaring at her accusingly. The four friends were sitting at their usual table in the cafeteria having dinner. "Um ..."

"What could be more important than accessorizing for the Spring Fling?" Lani folded her arms over her chest. "You're not still obsessing over the idea that there's some kind of plot against Ms. Carmichael, are you?"

Dylan shrugged. "Sort of," she admitted.

At that moment Patience wandered up to their table holding her dinner tray. "Did someone say Ms. Carmichael?" she asked. "You guys must have heard the news, then."

"What news?" Lani asked.

"Oh! Didn't you hear?" Patience widened her carefully lined eyes in mock surprise. "Some of the important alumni aren't too thrilled with the way the jumping teams are doing since Ms. Carmichael took over. Clare Houlder's mother, for instance. She's afraid we're going to lose the All Schools Jumping Trophy this year, and she's not happy about it."

"Who cares what Mrs. Houlder thinks?" Dylan snapped, annoyed by Patience's smug little smile.

"A lot of people," Patience replied. "Starting with everyone who uses all that super-fancy language lab equipment she donated last year. . . . All I can say is I'd hate to get on her bad side. I'd even hate to be *related* to anyone on her bad side." She shot Dylan an extra little smirk. "Oops! There's Lynsey. See you later, girls."

Dylan gritted her teeth as Patience scurried off. "Ugh. I think I just lost my appetite." Patience had been one of her least favorite people at Chestnut Hill ever since the time she'd tattled on Dylan for going down to the stable at night, and she didn't mind who knew it.

"You shouldn't let her get to you so much, Dylan." Honey stirred her soup to cool it. "You know she'll say anything to get attention. I'm sure it's all just a silly rumor."

"I know. You're right." Dylan took a deep breath, determined not to let Patience — or Clare and the Complainers, for that matter — ruin her weekend. She had already spent all day bouncing back and forth between excitement over the upcoming dance and worry over the Ali situation. Her friends had done their best to convince her that she was worried for nothing, but as much as she wanted to believe them, she couldn't quite banish that scene in the barn the previous evening from her mind. "Luckily I know the perfect thing to distract me — shopping!"

Unfortunately, that was not to be. "I'm sorry, Dylan," Ms. Herson said when Dylan stopped by the next morning to sign out for the trip into town. "No Cheney Falls for you today. You need to stay on campus and rest up this weekend. You don't want to risk getting sick again."

"What?" Dylan could hardly believe her ears. "But I'm totally better!"

The housemother shook her head. "Even if I believed that, we have to follow the rules," she said kindly. "And the rule is, no gym class, no riding, and no outside trips for a week after a stay in the Sick Suite."

"Well, then maybe I need to petition for a rule change," Dylan said, only half joking. Chestnut Hill encouraged its students to practice active democracy, which meant there was an official petition form available from the school secretary at all times. Any student could sign out a form and circulate the petition among her fellow students to gain support for a particular project or to protest a rule or decision. Dylan was always threatening to take out a petition against the serving of collard greens in the cafeteria, though so far she'd never followed through.

"I'm afraid there's not enough time to gather signatures before the first bus leaves at ten," Ms. Herson said with a hint of a smile. "But never mind, at least you should be all better by next weekend's Spring Fling."

"True. But I'll have nothing to wear," Dylan said miserably.

When her friends heard what the housemother had said, they immediately offered to stay behind with her.

"It won't be any fun going into town without you, Dyl," Lani said. "Especially since Mal's and Honey's boy-friends are stuck at St. Kits this weekend. I mean, what will I do for entertainment?"

"We can totally stay," Malory agreed, ignoring Lani's teasing reference to Caleb and Josh. "How will I pick out a dress without your style savvy?"

"No, don't you dare stay because of me!" Dylan pro-tested immediately. She knew Malory had been looking forward to the shopping trip even more than the others. One of her aunts had sent her some money as an early Easter present, which she planned to spend on a new outfit for the dance. "Why should we all wallow in my misery?"

"But . . ." Honey began.

"No, no, no!" Dylan insisted, cutting her off. "Trust me, it will make me feel even worse if you stay. Just promise me you guys'll help Mal find something that will make Caleb speechless." She bit her lip wistfully, think-ing of all the fun she would be missing. Then, noticing that her friends still looked uncertain, she grinned. "*And* promise you'll buy me lots of candy to make me feel bet-ter when you get back!"

Once the others had left for the bus stop, Dylan wan-dered down toward the stable, taking a shortcut across the grassy lawn behind Adams instead of walking on the path. If she couldn't be in town having fun with her friends, at least she could distract herself by giving Morello a good grooming.

She was surprised to see someone jumping a pony in the dressage arena. When she got a little closer, she recognized Lynsey and Bluegrass. There were just two jumps set up, a pair of fairly low verticals set about four strides apart. Beneath her GPA, Lynsey's face wore an expression of intense focus; even when Dylan stopped by the rail to watch, Lynsey didn't seem to notice.

She clucked to Bluegrass, who trotted briskly toward the first obstacle. However, a stride or two out he broke into a canter.

"No!" Lynsey cried. "That's not right. . . ."

She pulled her pony out of the line and circled to try again. This time Bluegrass stayed at a trot, but lurched rather awkwardly over the first fence and landed at a confused, half-trot, half-canter gait. When Lynsey pushed him on, he threw his head up and charged at the second fence, leaving the ground way too early and clipping the top rail with his hind feet.

Dylan decided to make herself scarce before Lynsey noticed she had an audience. Quickly skirting the end of the arena while Lynsey was turning Bluegrass back toward the line, she hurried into the barn.

Inside, she found stable hands Kelly and Sarah busy turning out the stalled horses and ponies to enjoy the springlike day. Dylan volunteered to help immediately. She might not be able to ride yet, but Ms. Herson hadn't said anything about *leading* a pony!

On her way back from taking Morello to his turnout, she passed the jumping arena, which was on the opposite side of the barns from the dressage ring. There was a private lesson going on in the arena — Anita Demarco was jumping her horse, Prince of Thieves, through a course under the watchful eye of Ms. Phillips — but that wasn't what caught Dylan's attention. A tall, poised-looking woman in her mid-thirties was standing by the fence watching Anita's ride.

Isn't that Ms. Mitchell? she thought, surprised to recognize the woman from Allbright's. *What in the world is she doing here?*

Dylan was never one to let shyness keep her from satisfying her curiosity. She walked over to the woman with a polite smile on her face.

"Hi, there," she said. "My name's Dylan. You're Ms. Mitchell from Allbrights, right? Can I help you out with something?"

Elizabeth Mitchell returned her smile. "How nice of you, Dylan," she said. "But I'm fine. I'm a little early for a meeting with Dr. Starling, and I thought the stable would be a much more pleasant place to wait than anywhere else."

"Oh, okay." Dylan kept the smile on her face, but her mind was racing. Why would Ms. Mitchell have a meeting with the school principal?

Ms. Mitchell was looking at Dylan curiously. "Aren't you Ms. Carmichael's niece?" she asked. "I believe I saw you ride at last weekend's show, yes? You were on that flashy new pinto pony."

"Yeah, that was me," Dylan said. "His name's Morello. He belongs to my aunt — she brought him with her from Kentucky."

"Well, you make a good team. You adjusted his stride perfectly before the in-and-out, and you also handled him well when he looked at the wall."

Dylan couldn't help being flattered, not to mention impressed by how much the woman had noticed and remembered about her ride. But she almost immediately felt disloyal.

"Ms. Carmichael did a great job preparing us for the show," she said.

Just then there was the clatter of hooves on the path behind them. "Ms. Mitchell!"

Clare Houlder was dragging Sancha along at the end of her reins. Contrary to her usual intense expression, Clare's face wore a big, sincerely excited grin that actually made her look quite pretty and relaxed.

"Clare!" Ms. Mitchell seemed equally pleased. "I'm so glad to see you. I thought we'd get a chance to catch up on Saturday, but I was surprised to find you weren't competing."

Dylan winced. *Great,* she thought. *As if Clare needs to be reminded she didn't make this year's senior team!*

"Yes," Clare said after a moment. "Um, I've been riding a new horse lately." She waved a hand toward Sancha, who was nibbling at the dangling leather reins. "I guess we weren't quite ready for the team yet."

Ms. Mitchell nodded thoughtfully. "Sancha is a good choice for you," she said. "You should learn a lot from each other."

Dylan couldn't resist staying to watch as Anita rode out of the ring, and Clare began her private lesson with Ms. Phillips. Ms. Mitchell was still watching, too.

"Sancha looks well," she commented quietly to Dylan as Clare pushed the light bay mare into a steady trot. "She's always been a bit high strung, but she makes up for it by being a real trier."

Dylan nodded. "She seems cool."

They fell silent for a few minutes, watching as Clare completed her warmup and then jumped a few practice fences. Dylan could tell that the older girl was trying hard to impress her former coach. She was really working at keeping Sancha focused and together, and it showed.

After watching the pair move on to jumping a course or two, Ms. Mitchell checked her watch. "I'd better move on if I don't want to be late for that meeting." She smiled at Dylan. "It's been nice talking with you, Dylan. Best of luck with your riding."

"Thanks." Dylan smiled back. Even though she felt she ought to dislike Elizabeth Mitchell on principle, how could she dislike someone who cared so deeply about horses and riding and her students?

Ms. Mitchell waited for a pause in the lesson before calling out a good-bye to Clare. Then she headed up the path at a brisk walk toward the Old House.

A little while later, Dylan was re-bedding Morello's freshly cleaned stall when Clare returned from her lesson. Her friend Chloe had appeared, and the two girls were chattering eagerly as Clare led Sancha down the aisle. The big bay mare had the stall directly across from Morello's, so Dylan could hear every word as Clare hooked Sancha to the cross-ties right between the two stalls to untack her.

"So what do you think she's doing here?" Chloe asked, her voice squeaking with excitement. "Do you think —"

"That she's here about for her old job?" Clare finished for her. "You must be a mind reader. That's exactly why I think she's here!"

Dylan was tired of overhearing so much catty chit-chat, yet she really didn't have the energy to confront Clare and the rest of the scheme team now. "But we already have Ms. Carmichael," Chloe said. "What are the chances that they'd let her go?"

"Gee, I don't know," Clare said sarcastically. "I'd say a better question is, what are our chances of winning the All Schools Trophy with Ali Carmichael here?"

Dylan took a breath and waited for Chloe's answer, but it was Clare who spoke again.

"We have a winning tradition at Chestnut Hill, and I think the administration knows what they have to do to make sure it stays that way."

CHAPTER EIGHT

For the next few minutes Dylan tried to distract herself by giving Morello's saddle a good scrubbing. But it was no use. What if Ms. Mitchell really had come to Chestnut Hill to talk about getting her job back?

Eventually she gave up on her tack cleaning and went in search of Ali. She found her in the comfortable, cluttered stable office, bent over some paperwork.

"Hi. What are you doing?" Dylan said, rapping lightly on the edge of the open doorway as she stepped inside.

Ali glanced up at her, rubbing her temple with one hand. "Oh, hi, Dylan. I was just looking over the tryout list to see who can replace Sara on the team for the next few shows."

Dylan's heart stopped. "What?" she cried. "What happened to Mischief?"

"Relax," Ali cut her off, raising both hands. "Nothing

happened. He's still going to be okay. But that stone bruise was pretty bad, and Sara doesn't want to take any chances."

For a second, Dylan was relieved. Then she realized this was still bad news. "But we need her on the team," she protested. "Sara and Mischief always pull in one of the top scores!"

"That's true," Ali said. "But Sara wants to make sure Mischief is back to one hundred percent before asking him to jump that much. His long-term soundness is more important to her than a handful of ribbons."

"But the vet said it might only be a couple of weeks," Dylan said. "And without Mischief, there's no way we'll win the All Schools Trophy this year."

"Mischief isn't what will hold this team back from winning that trophy." Ali's voice had suddenly gone stern. "If he did, we wouldn't deserve it, anyway."

"Um, okay." Dylan tried to find another way out of the problem. Chestnut Hill could not come up short at the next show as well. "Why doesn't Sara just ride a different horse for the next few shows? I'm sure she could do great on Sancha or maybe even Quincy. . . ."

"Sara's not like that," Ali replied. "She's competitive, of course, but the teamwork with her horse is the most important thing to her. I don't think she'd want to compete on another horse." She glanced at the list in front of her and scratched her ear. "I've already moved Helena up to full member," she said. "Now I'm just trying to decide who to bring in as the new reserve rider."

Each of Chestnut Hill's jumping teams had four full members plus one reserve. Dylan was the reserve rider for the junior team, while Helena Wright rode reserve for the seniors. In the All Schools shows, however, all five members got to ride, since the scores were computed on a percentage rather than points basis. That meant it was an advantage to have a full roster of five riders for those shows.

Dylan leaned closer to peer at the list on the desk. "Well, Emma Swaisland is a good rider," she said. "Too bad she practically hyperventilates anytime she even thinks about going in the show ring." Ali gave Dylan an appraising look. "And Charlotte Bauer can't do it now that she started volunteering on weekends. . . . Clare Houlder! Yes! You should sign up Clare," Dylan blurted out when she spotted the next name on the list.

Her aunt glanced at her in surprise, but Dylan hardly noticed. Her mind was racing.

It's not like I want to see Clare get what she wants, she thought. *But in a way, it's the perfect solution. Ali puts her on the team, and presto! All Clare's complaints are over. Without Clare and her friends fanning the flames, everyone else will forget there was ever a problem, especially if Ali gets over this new drill-sergeant-instructor thing soon. Besides, Clare's a pretty good rider — probably the best out of anybody who's not already on the team. . . .*

But Ali was shaking her head. "I know Clare is a talented rider," she said. "And she had a good tryout at the beginning of the year. But those aren't the only requirements to be a part of the team. Anita Demarco did just as well. They both had four faults in the jump-off, so I think I'm going to give Anita the chance."

"But . . ." Dylan began.

She quickly stopped herself. Ali had that look on her face — the look that meant she was in Riding Director mode, not cool, relaxed, tell-me-anything aunt mode.

"Okay," Dylan said instead. "Well, it was just a thought. See you later."

She hurried off before her aunt could notice the distressed look on her face. Because if Clare had been upset that she hadn't made the team the first time, Dylan couldn't even imagine how she was going to react when she found out that Ali had passed her over again.

"We're back!" Lani cried, leaping into Dylan's room with a flourish. She had shopping bags hanging off each arm, and a new Motif 56 leather belt draped around her neck.

Honey and Malory followed her into the room in a more dignified manner. Both of them were clutching shopping bags, too.

Dylan had been lying on her bed working on some makeup math problems from when she was sick. "It's about time!" she cried, sitting up and shoving away her homework. "I thought you guys would never get back."

Malory set down her bags beside Honey's bed. "I wish you'd been there with us, Dylan," she said. "These two aren't much help when it comes to clothes shopping."

Honey looked insulted. "I beg your pardon? Who found you those cute earrings at seventy-five percent off?"

"Okay, okay." Malory laughed as Honey gave her a sharp poke in the shoulder. "I take it back. You're a clothes-shopping genius. It's only Lani who's hopeless!"

Lani grinned good-naturedly. "Guilty as charged. And proud of it!"

Dylan knew the others were just kidding around. Lani always dressed well, but she was a lot more casual than the fashionistas of Chestnut Hill. Still, she had a singular — if somewhat Western-infused — style, and even managed to start a mini-trend. Since the Rodeo Day fund-raiser Lani had helped plan recently, Dylan had noticed a definite increase in the number of girls trekking around campus in cowboy boots.

"So what did you get?" she asked all three of her friends, eyeing their bags with interest. "Is this all for the dance? Or did you stock up for all of next year's parties, too?"

"Oh, you know. We just wanted to cover our bases." Lani dumped one of her bags out onto Honey's bed. "I spent more on jeans and stuff than my dress, but you've got to see what Malory bought."

Malory shook her head, but Honey grabbed her friend's bag and pulled out a shimmering length of fabric. Honey held it up in front of Malory, who smiled shyly as Dylan let out a wolf whistle. The dress was made of fluid midnight-blue velvet, which brought out the brighter blue of Malory's eyes. Even without seeing it on her, Dylan could tell that the draped bodice, slim straps, and full skirt would look incredible on Malory's slender figure.

"Oh, it's so cool!" Dylan said. "It's understated but stunning — just like you, Mal."

"I really like it," Malory agreed. "Of course, it's not a one-of-a-kind designer exclusive like some people will be wearing." She shot a glance toward Lynsey's part of the room.

"Who cares?" Dylan said. "You don't have to rely on expensive labels to look good, and it's hardly a competition." Voicing the word *competition* jogged Dylan's memory. In all the excitement over the shoppers' return, Dylan had almost forgotten her big news, and she couldn't wait to hear her friends' take on it. "Guess who was here at Chestnut Hill today?" She paused for effect. "Elizabeth Mitchell."

"Who?" Honey wrinkled her brow, seeming a bit confused at the sudden change of topic.

"Ms. Mitchell from Allbright's?" Malory asked at almost the same time. "Why was she here?"

"She said she had a meeting with Dr. Starling," Dylan reported. "And get this — the buzz around the barn was that she was here about her old job!"

Honey still looked confused. "What? But we have Ms. Carmichael now."

"Exactly," Dylan said.

Malory dropped her dress on Honey's bed. "Since when are you so quick to believe barn gossip, Dylan?" she asked. "It's easy for people to speculate, but it's not like there's any real evidence."

Dylan shook her head. "I don't think you guys are getting this," she said. "Liz Mitchell was here on campus. Meeting with Dr. Starling. A week after we had one of the stinkiest shows in history. What else could explain it?"

"Lots of things," Malory said. "It could be something about the All Schools league. Or she could be trying to buy one of our horses for Allbrights. Or maybe it's nothing to do with school or riding at all — they've known each other a long time, right?"

"I guess." Dylan felt a twinge of annoyance that her friends weren't taking her more seriously. "But what if you're wrong? What if the gossip is right this time, and she really is here to talk about getting her job back? What if Clare's mom really is all up in arms about the show? What if Ali's job really is in danger?"

"Then there's not much we can do about it, is there?" Honey said with a wry smile and a shrug. "Dr. Starling isn't likely to consult us about faculty hiring."

Dylan opened her mouth to respond. Then she closed it again, feeling bleak as she realized Honey was right.

"I don't know why I have to do so much extra studying just because you're still trying to impress your parents with straight A-pluses," Dylan complained as she and Lani walked into the library the next day.

Located near the center of campus, the library's contemporary octagonal architecture stood out against the classic antebellum lines of the Old House and the school chapel, which stood just across the lawn, as well as the newer but more traditional design of the dorms, student center, and most of the other buildings. Dylan had always liked the library — she thought of the building as a rebel of sorts, like a girl wearing cool jeans and a leather jacket to a debutante ball.

"You should thank me for dragging you here," Lani said as they passed the checkout desk in the sun-filled lobby area. "You missed most of last week's classes, remember? It's time to do some makeup cramming, baby!"

Dylan made a face, but she knew her friend was right. The study carrels on the main floor were crowded, as they always were on Sunday afternoons when many students suddenly remembered they had tests to study for and papers to finish before Monday morning. But the two girls soon found a double carrel along the back wall. At one of the long library tables nearby, Dylan noticed that Jessica Jones had an immense number of books, papers, and charts spread out in front of her. The only other person sitting at her table was Ansty Van Sweetering, who had a single textbook in front of her. The two older girls seemed to be doing more gossiping and giggling than studying, but Dylan did her best to tune them out as she opened her French textbook.

Fifteen minutes later, her head was spinning. "I can't keep these stupid French verb conjugations straight," she grumbled. "I wonder if I should e-mail Henri for help."

Lani glanced at her curiously. "Have you heard from *Monsieur Henri* lately?" she asked in an exaggerated French accent.

"Not much." Dylan shrugged. "He e-mailed me once while I was sick. But I wrote to him yesterday about the whole Ali situation, and I haven't heard back from him yet. I should probably —" She paused as soon as she'd heard the name "Liz Mitchell" drifting over from where Jessica and Ansty were sitting.

"What's the —" Lani began, but she fell quiet when Dylan gestured toward the older girls.

". . . and if you ask me, this could be just what the teams need," Jessica was saying, her voice growing louder with each word. "Otherwise we can kiss that All Schools Trophy good-bye."

"Wow." Ansty tugged thoughtfully at her straight blonde bangs. "I can't believe this is for real."

"Believe it." Jessica's eyes were gleaming. "At least someone's taking action about this!"

"Action?" Dylan murmured. "What's that supposed to mean?"

She leaned forward to hear more. But Jessica had lowered her voice again. All Dylan could make out as the older girl whispered eagerly to Ansty were the words "office," "signing," and "lots of support."

Dylan frowned. At first she'd assumed Jessica was talking about Ms. Mitchell's meeting with Dr. Starling. But this sounded like something more than that.

A moment later, Jessica glanced at her watch and let out a cry of alarm. "I've got to go," she exclaimed, gathering up her masses of study material. "I told Jillian I'd meet her at the barn ten minutes ago."

As soon as Jessica had disappeared out the library door, Dylan pushed her chair back. "I'm going to talk to Ansty," she told Lani. "She's usually pretty nice, even to us seventh-grade peons. Maybe she'll tell me what's really going on here."

"Wait, Dyl," Lani began. "Are you sure you —"

Dylan didn't wait around to hear any more. She was tired of wondering and speculating and worrying without knowing anything for sure. Marching over to Ansty's table, she plopped down in the chair just vacated by Jessica. "Hi," she said.

Ansty looked surprised to see her. "Dylan," she said. Was it Dylan's imagination or was her voice a little less friendly than usual? "What's up?"

"That's what I want to know." Dylan wasn't sure if she should beseech Ansty to confess or try to bully it out of her. Dylan crossed her arms over her chest and stared at the older girl. "What were you and Jessica talking about just now?"

Ansty's pale complexion immediately went pink. "I don't know what you mean," she mumbled. She glanced at her wrist, which was bare. "Oops! Look at the time. I have to go, too." Picking up her book, she rushed away without a backward glance.

"What did she say?" Lani asked when Dylan stomped back to their carrel.

"Nothing," Dylan replied grimly. "But that told me everything I need to know."

CHAPTER NINE

"Ms. Walsh, could you do me a favor?"

Dylan looked up from stuffing her music notebook back into her pack. Dr. Jeremy Hurst, the music teacher, was standing by her front row desk. Tall and thin, with wispy graying hair and a stoop to his posture, Dr. Hurst was soft-spoken and passionate about his subject. Even though she had a singing voice that Lani had once compared to a foghorn, music was one of Dylan's favorite classes, thanks to the teacher's relaxed but creative teaching style and his enthusiasm for her efforts on the violin.

"Sure, Dr. Hurst," she said. "What's up?"

The teacher held out an envelope with an apologetic smile. "This needs to go to the main office," he said. "But I have my juniors coming in any moment. Would you mind dropping this for me in Dr. Starling's in-box on your way to lunch?"

Dylan took the envelope and tucked it into the outside

pocket of her backpack. "Sure, no prob," she said. "See you Wednesday, Dr. H."

After telling her friends she'd catch up with them in the cafeteria, Dylan veered off the path and cut across the lawn toward the Old House. In the doorway to Dr. Starling's office suite, she almost ran into Ms. Danby, the principal's assistant.

"Oh! Excuse me," Dylan mumbled. She wasn't easily intimidated, but Ms. Danby was one person who could make her feel tongue-tied. Slim, blonde, and utterly efficient, the woman had a way of staring at students as if she could read every thought in their heads.

"Yes?" Ms. Danby paused and stared down at Dylan. "May I help you, Ms. Walsh?"

Impressed as always by the way the assistant knew every student's name on sight, Dylan scrambled for the envelope. "Dr. Hurst wanted me to leave this for Dr. Starling."

Ms. Danby waved a hand toward her spacious, tidy desk just inside the office waiting room. "Leave it in my in-box," she said. "I'll take care of it when I get back."

As the brisk *click-clack* of Ms. Danby's high-heeled footsteps faded down the hall outside, Dylan hurried over to the desk. She had just remembered that the cafeteria was serving pizza that day for lunch, and she hoped her friends made sure to snag her a slice of pepperoni before it was all gone and she got stuck with plain cheese.

She dropped the envelope in the in-box and started to turn away. Then she stopped short as her brain caught up with her eyes. Was she going crazy, or had she just spotted Clare Houlder's name atop the neat stack of papers just behind the in-box?

Turning, she craned over the in-box for a better look. She gasped. Sure enough, there was Clare's name . . . at the top of the sign-out list for the student petition form!

Dylan rushed around the desk, hoping against hope that Ms. Danby didn't return suddenly and find her back there. Grabbing the list, which was attached to a clipboard, she flipped through it with her hands shaking. But there was nothing anywhere noting the topic of Clare's proposed petition, only her name and the date of the request, which was that day.

But it's not like Clare's likely to start a petition requesting more herbal tea in the cafeteria or something, Dylan thought in dismay. She remembered what Jessica had said in the library — something about "signing" and "taking action." *This must mean that Clare was totally serious about trying to bring Ms. Mitchell back!*

"Miss Walsh! What are you doing back there?"

Dylan gulped, glancing up at Ms. Danby, who was glaring at her from the doorway. "Er — I was just looking for — for this petition sign-out," she said, thinking fast. "I — I remembered after I got here that I wanted to, um, petition for — for more herbal tea choices in the cafeteria."

Ms. Danby looked suspicious, but she nodded. "Very well," she said. "However, I would have preferred you waited until I returned. This is not a self-serve office."

"Sorry," Dylan said meekly, hurrying around to the front of the desk.

Though she was impatient to fly off to the cafeteria to tell her friends what she'd just learned, Dylan forced herself to wait patiently while Ms. Danby Xeroxed a new petition form for her. "Add your name and the date to the sign-out, please," the woman told Dylan, who was still holding the clipboard.

Dylan did as she said. As she added her name just below Clare's, she suddenly had an idea — one so inspired, so perfect, that her hands started shaking again. As Ms. Danby released her, she stuffed the petition form into her bag and forced herself to walk calmly out of the office and down the hall. But as soon as she was outside, she burst into a run.

☙

. . . and so I'm sure this is her way of trying to get rid of Ali." Dylan paused to take what felt like her first deep breath since leaving Dr. Starling's office. "We have to do something!"

"Okay," Lani said. "I admit that doesn't sound good —

Clare isn't exactly the student council, save-the-whales type. But maybe we'd better make sure what she's up to before we jump off the deep end."

Malory nodded. "I agree. Besides, there's no way a student petition will make Ms. Carmichael lose her job."

"Not even with Mrs. Houlder influencing Dr. Starling behind the scenes?" Dylan grimaced, poking at the slice of pepperoni pizza on the plate in front of her to see if it was cool enough to eat. "I can't believe you guys still don't believe there's a real problem here. What's it going to take to convince you? Waving good-bye as Ali drives off back to Kentucky with Morello and Quincy?"

"Don't have a stroke, Dylan," Lani said. "None of us wants to see that. Obviously."

"Well, then we'd better all do something about it," Dylan said. "Luckily I already have a great idea."

"What is it?" Honey asked.

"We're going to start a petition of our own. I already signed out the form. We can get everyone to sign it saying they want Ali to stay no matter what. I'm sure we can get more signatures than Clare and the conspiracy crew!"

Honey looked troubled. "I don't know, Dylan," she said. "If you do something like that, Clare and the others would definitely find out about it."

"So what?" Dylan glared at her. "I'm willing to stand up for what I believe in. Aren't you?"

"Easy, Dylan," Malory put in. "Just because you're upset is no reason to take it out on Honey."

Dylan rounded on her, suddenly remembering her little rendezvous with Lynsey. "Look, we all know Honey's a total pacifist," she said. "But what's *your* excuse, Mal? Has Lynsey tried to convince you that Ali has to go?"

Lani gasped. "Dylan!" she cried. "I can't believe you said that!"

Malory's face turned bright red. "I can't either," she said, her voice tight and cold. "I know it's hard for you to not be in on every little secret, Dylan. But I thought you knew me better than that."

Dylan already felt a pang of guilt about what she'd said, but it was too late to back down now. "I thought I did, too," she retorted. "But I also thought the Malory I knew didn't keep secrets from her best friends anymore."

Without another word, Malory got up and strode off. Dylan bit her lip, realizing she might have gone too far. When she'd first met Malory, Dylan had been bothered by the other girl's reserved manner, especially once she'd suspected that Malory was keeping secrets about herself — secrets that had turned out to involve nothing more than her riding scholarship and her father's humble economic status. After that rough beginning, it had taken them a while to trust each other. Had she just blown that trust?

"Mal!" Honey cried, casting Dylan a reproachful

glance before jumping out of her seat and hurrying after Malory.

"Nice work, Walsh." Lani's voice dripped with sarcasm. She picked up a loose blob of cheese and popped it in her mouth. "Way to make a bad situation even worse."

Dylan glared at her, torn between guilt and annoyance. "Aren't you even a little bit curious about what Lynsey had to say to Malory?"

"Sure, I guess." Lani shrugged. "But you know how Lynsey is. She thinks everything she does is super-important classified information. She was probably just trying to convince Malory to braid for her at the next show. Or maybe she's looking for help in math class."

"Lynsey always gets A's in math," Dylan countered.

Lani rolled her eyes. "You know what I mean. My point is, we shouldn't assume it's something bad just because Lynsey's involved and swore Mal to secrecy."

"Are you clinical? That's exactly why we *should* assume it's something bad! Since when is Lynsey *ever* involved in anything not-bad?" Dylan's mind was already racing with new possibilities. "Especially now that we know about this petition thing. What if Lynsey's trying to convince Mal to go along with it?"

"Yeah, right," Lani said. "I'm sure that's what it was — Lynsey was promising Mal all kinds of show-ring glory if she signs the stupid petition and helps Ms. Mitchell come back."

Dylan's eyes widened. "Oh, I didn't even think of that!" she cried. "You could totally be right! Lynsey knows Mal's an awesome rider, and she —"

"Hold it, Walsh." Lani held up her hand. "I was kidding. For one thing, as long as Mal's riding Tybalt, there are no guarantees of anything in the show ring. How they do depends on his mood that day. I mean, we all know Mal's a great rider. But even she can't finesse it too much when he spooks at a terrifying pile of horse poop right in front of the judge!"

Dylan smiled in spite of herself. Tybalt had done exactly that at a show earlier that semester. "Okay, you have a point there," she admitted, tapping her spoon on the table. "But Lynsey isn't exactly Ms. Detail. She might not think of that. See, this is why we have to do my petition idea! We can't let the bad guys get ahead of us on this."

"Look," Lani said with a sigh. "If I agree to help you with this petition thing, will you promise to apologize to Malory and Honey for all the obnoxious stuff you just said?"

"Sure!" Dylan said immediately. "No problem!"

"And one other thing," Lani said. "You have to lay off trying to badger Mal into telling you what Lynsey wanted to talk to her about."

"Whatever." Dylan still didn't understand why Lani and Honey weren't more curious about that. But it didn't matter. The important thing was to get her friends on board with the petition.

She felt new energy and hope pulsing through her. Sitting around worrying about what might happen never did anyone any good. But now they were taking action, which had always been Dylan's specialty. Her heart pounded as she thought about the job they had in front of them. The countercampaign had begun!

CHAPTER TEN

"Oh, Morello!" Dylan cried, impulsively stopping in the doorway to give her tacked-up pony a hug as she led him out of the barn that afternoon. "I've missed riding you so much!"

Lynsey, who had to stop Bluegrass abruptly to keep him from walking into Morello's rear end, rolled her eyes. "Really, Dylan," she said. "It's not like you were gone for a year. Or like he missed having your big butt in the saddle last week, for that matter."

Dylan ignored Lynsey's grumbling and gave Morello one more hug before leading him on toward the mounting block. To her surprise, she had a little trouble swinging on and over — her legs felt like jelly.

"Wow," she said aloud, bending over to adjust a stirrup. "I didn't know you could lose all your riding muscles in, like, a week! Morello, you'll have to take care of me today, okay, buddy?"

She shot a glance at Lynsey, expecting another sarcastic comment. The two of them were the only ones outside so far; the rest of their seventh-grade intermediate riding class was still tacking up in the barn. For a second she was tempted to confront Lynsey about her secret meeting with Malory. After all, Lani hadn't made her promise anything about badgering Lynsey. . . .

But Lynsey wasn't paying attention to her anymore. She was adjusting Bluegrass's noseband, a slight frown creasing her forehead. At that moment Lani emerged leading Colorado, with Malory and Tybalt right behind her. Dylan waved to them, forgetting all about Lynsey's cranky behavior. She'd lived up to her promise to Lani and apologized to the other two girls. Both had accepted immediately, though Dylan couldn't help noticing that Malory was still acting a little distant.

Before long the lesson started. By the time she finished warming up, Dylan's legs already felt weak and wobbly. But she pushed herself through it, determined to get back in riding shape as quickly as possible.

Fortunately Morello was in an agreeable mood. He stayed forward and steady through the flat portion of the ride, and once they started jumping he pricked his ears forward and handled each obstacle with controlled enthusiasm.

Bluegrass, on the other hand, didn't seem to be having such a good day. The first time Lynsey aimed him toward the three-jump warm-up line Ms. Carmichael had set up, the handsome blue roan pony balked and spun out, shaking his head and threatening to buck.

"Bring him around again, Lynsey," Ms. Carmichael said. "This time, focus more on keeping him forward. Give him a tap with your crop a few strides out and then keep pushing if you feel him suck back."

Lynsey brought Bluegrass to a halt and shook her head. "Using the crop that way doesn't work with Blue," she said. "He's trained to lengthen his stride if I tap him, and that will mess up our spot."

"All right." Ms. Carmichael's voice remained calm. "I understand that. But the important thing is to get him over the jump to start with. And these jumps are low enough that the spot doesn't matter much. So please just give it a try, all right?"

"No!" Lynsey's voice rose in frustration. "I told you, that won't work! It'll just confuse him and mess up his training!"

Ms. Carmichael sighed. "Fine," she said. "If you'd rather not try it again right now, take your place at the end of the line. Heidi? You're up next."

Dylan stared worriedly at Lynsey as she rode past. Bluegrass was almost always pitch-perfect in class, especially when it came to jumping. First Ali, then her friends, now even Bluegrass . . . What was going on with everyone at Chestnut Hill these days?

❧

"Ready to go?" Lani asked forty minutes later, pausing in front of Morello's stall.

Dylan looked up from picking a few strands of hay out of Morello's tail. "I'll catch up to you guys in a minute," she said. "I want to make sure I give him the total spa experience since he took such good care of me today."

"Okay." Lani smiled and gave Morello a rub on the nose. "See you back at the dorm."

Dylan heard her friends moving off down the aisle. "Just you and me, boy," she murmured to Morello, sighing with contentment. For just a few minutes, it was nice to forget about plots and petitions and schoolwork and everything else, and instead focus all her attention on her favorite pony in the world.

But only a couple of minutes passed before she heard Lani's voice calling out her name from the end of the aisle. Stepping to the front of the stall, she looked out and saw her friend rushing toward her, red-faced and breathless.

"You won't believe what's happening out there," Lani cried. "Come see!"

Not giving Dylan a chance to ask any questions, she turned and raced off. Dylan let herself out of the stall and followed, curious and a little worried.

Outside, she saw Honey and Malory standing at the

gate watching the eleventh-grade advanced lesson going on in the ring. Dr. Starling was there, too, leaning on the fence as Ms. Carmichael called out instructions to the riders from the center of the ring. At first Dylan wasn't sure what she was supposed to be seeing. Lani glanced at her, reading her confusion.

"Just wait," Lani said grimly, nodding toward the junior riders.

Dylan wandered over to join her friends, watching as Clare Houlder trotted Sancha toward a four-fence gymnastic exercise. The mare's mouth gaped as she trotted over a placing pole and neared the first jump, a cross rail. She jumped the obstacle, but tossed her head irritably as she landed at a jerky half trot, half canter.

"Yikes," Dylan hissed to her friends. "If she doesn't get moving, she's going to . . ."

She let her voice trail off as Sancha lurched over the second element, a vertical, from a ridiculously close spot, and wound up taking the rail down with her front legs. "That didn't work!" Clare, who was spinning her horse out of the combination, cried in the direction of Aunt Ali. "The stupid placing pole is in the wrong spot or something. Are you sure you paced it off right, Ms. Carmichael?"

"The spacing is fine, Clare," Ali replied. "The whole point of this grid is to work on a more forward canter between obstacles. As I told you, you'll need a strong trot going in so she'll canter on landing. And make sure you give her a release over the jumps."

Dylan rolled her eyes. "Yeah," she murmured to her friends. "Didn't we all learn to release in, oh, our first week of jumping?"

Clare took her place at the end of the line, still grumbling under her breath. The next rider up was Colette Prior, who was riding Kingfisher, the talented but easy-going bright bay Warmblood. The pair trotted briskly over the placing pole. Over the cross rail, Dylan saw the rider's leg slip back, which seemed strange — Colette had near-perfect equitation and almost never lost position, not even over jumps three times the size of that cross rail.

Kingfisher landed with his head up and bolted forward. Instead of the two long strides he was supposed to fit in before the vertical, the gelding's too-fast stride meant the best he could manage was an awkward one and a half.

Dylan's heart stopped as she realized what was happening. "They're doing it on purpose, aren't they?" she whispered. "Kingfisher would never do that on his own — Colette threw him over the jump so he'd miss the striding."

Lani nodded, her brown eyes flashing fire as Kingfisher crashed through the final two elements, snorting and rolling his eyes. "It's Clare and her two little sidekicks,

Colette and Chloe," she said. "They started up over the warm-up line, and now they're just getting worse. Chloe actually got Hardy to do a little buck during her turn!"

"They know Dr. Starling is watching, and they're taking advantage," Malory added.

"There's no way she'll fall for that, is there?" Honey asked worriedly. "I mean, she saw Anita and Kelsey go through that grid first with hardly any trouble at all."

"Let's hope," Malory said, though she didn't sound optimistic.

In the ring, Ms. Carmichael finished resetting the jumps. "All right," she said. "Let's have Clare, Chloe, and Colette give it another try. I realize this grid is more challenging than most of the ones we've done in the past, but I know you're all more than capable of riding it well. So let's see some improvement, all right?"

This time Chloe and Hardy made it through the gymnastic without knocking anything down. But it wasn't a pretty ride — the stout chestnut gelding lept long for the first element, and put in extra strides for the next two before finally managing a decent jump over the last.

"Ugh!" Chloe announced as she trotted back toward the group. "That just didn't ride right at all."

"All right, if there's time you can try again," Ali said. "Clare? You're up."

Dylan watched in disbelief as Clare forced Sancha into

a fast, uncomposed trot. The horse ended up scrambling over the first fence and then was off stride for the next.

Clare pulled the mare to a halt right in the middle of the combination. "I just can't do this!" she complained, her tone high and forced. "If we're going to be expected to jump this particular exercise as it's set now, I don't feel comfortable or safe jumping anymore."

"Fine." Ali's voice was as calm as ever. "Walk her at the far end of the ring to cool her down, then take her back to the stable."

Clare turned away without another word, aiming her horse toward the empty end of the ring as instructed. As she passed the group, her back to Ali, she winked and grinned at Colette, who was just riding forward for her next turn.

Dylan's fingernails dug into her palms as she glared daggers at Clare and her friends. "They're totally faking this!" she hissed to her friends. "The Three C's — they're trying to make Ali look bad in front of you-know-who." She jerked her head in the direction of Dr. Starling.

"Easy," Lani murmured. "Dr. Starling had to see that nobody else in the class is having such serious problems with the exercise. She's not stupid."

"I know that." Knowing Dr. Starling was an experienced horsewoman made Dylan feel better for a second.

Then she glanced at the other students in the class. Kelsey Howett was staring at the gymnastic with a small frown on her face. Lizzie Walters looked worried as she glanced down the ring after Clare. And Anita Demarco and Helen Savage were whispering to each other from their horses' backs.

Dylan bit her lip as she noticed the girls' reactions. It looked like Clare's outburst was affecting more than Dr. Starling's opinion.

❧

"Ms. Walsh."

"Ms. Walsh?"

"*Ms. Walsh!*"

Dylan blinked and glanced up from her notebook, where she was doodling in the margins of her class notes. Her geography teacher, Mr. Westrop, was glaring at her with an annoyed expression on his normally friendly face. Across the aisle, Dylan noticed that Honey was shooting her an anxious look.

"Um . . . present?" she said weakly.

Mr. Westrop crossed his arms over his argyle sweater-vest, not looking amused. "Is it just taking you an extra long time to remember the capital of Ecuador, or were you hoping I'd assume you'd slipped into a coma and go on to the next person?" he asked. There were giggles from around the classroom, including one near-guffaw that Dylan was pretty sure had come from Patience, though she didn't dare turn around to look.

"The capital of Ecuador?" Dylan echoed. Luckily geography usually came easily to her, and she pulled the correct answer out of her brain. "Um, it's Quito."

"All right." With one last glare, the teacher moved on to the next desk.

Dylan slumped in her seat with a relieved sigh. It was Tuesday, and she was finding it harder and harder to concentrate in her classes. She and Lani had written up their pro-Ali petition the previous afternoon, and that morning they'd stood outside the student center before breakfast, collecting signatures. Dylan had been so adamant about collecting as many signatures as possible that she didn't even grab a bagel, so she was now feeling lightheaded. Meanwhile Honey still seemed skeptical of the whole petition idea, and Malory frowned and changed the subject whenever Dylan brought it up.

As much as Dylan hated to admit it, their lack of enthusiasm was already getting to her. It didn't help that only about one out of every four or five students she approached was willing to sign. It was no surprise that some of the non-riders weren't interested in getting involved with a riding issue, but Dylan was startled by the number of riders who refused to sign. Some openly favored Ms. Mitchell's return, while others didn't believe in interfering with faculty issues. But the most common reason Dylan heard was that Ms. Carmichael was being way too tough on all the riding classes lately. After listening to eighth-grader Leah Bates rant about the striding of the intermediate class's latest set of gymnastics, Dylan started to wonder if she was wasting her time. Why did Ali have to pick now of all times to play Dragon Lady? Didn't she even *want* to stay?

The only time such doom-and-gloom thoughts receded was when she remembered that the Spring Fling dance at St. Kits was less than five days away. Despite missing out on the Cheney Falls shopping trip, she'd managed to come up with a great outfit for the dance.

Thank goodness for the Fling, she told herself, gathering up her books as the teacher dismissed the class. *Otherwise I wouldn't have anything fun to think about these days at all!*

With a shiver of anticipation, she imagined dancing the night away with her schoolmates and their friends at St. Kits. She couldn't wait to see Caleb's reaction to Malory's new dress, and she and Lani were already coming up with devious ways to leave Honey and Josh alone together. Dylan's cousin Nat would be there, too, and hanging out with him was always a blast.

This dance could end up being the celebration of the semester, Dylan told herself. Her smile faded slightly as she left the classroom and noticed an old poster for the All Schools show hanging in the hallway. *I only hope that by Saturday, we all have something to celebrate.*

CHAPTER ELEVEN

"Hey, Tybalt," Dylan said, clicking her tongue at the bay pony so he wouldn't be startled as she passed him. He was standing in cross-ties in the stable aisle, all tacked up except for his bridle. "Does this mean Malory's around here somewhere?"

Besides Malory, only a few students ever rode Tybalt in lessons, and as far as Dylan knew, none of them were likely to put in any extra riding time on him outside of class. Bluegrass was in the next set of ties, also tacked up. Dylan gave him a friendly pat on the rump as she hurried past. It was Wednesday afternoon; classes had just let out, and she had stopped in at the barn for a quick visit with Morello before heading back to the dorm to meet up with Lani to tackle some homework.

But now that it seemed Malory might be there, she decided Lani could wait. Things were still a little tense between Dylan and Malory, and it was past time for them to have a talk.

She hurried into the tack room, skidding to a stop to avoid bumping into Malory, who was standing just inside the door. "There you are, Mal," Dylan blurted out before realizing her friend wasn't alone. "Oh, excuse me, Ms. Carmichael," she added.

Lynsey was in the room, too. "Do you mind?" she snapped at Dylan. "We're trying to have a conversation here."

Dylan looked from Lynsey to Malory to Ali and back again. She suddenly had the uncomfortable feeling that she'd just walked in on something private. "Is there an intermediate lesson I didn't hear about?" she tried, wondering if she might discover what was going on with this unlikely combination of people.

"No, Dylan," Ali said with a hint of exasperation. "The girls just wanted to go out on a trail ride."

"A trail ride?" Dylan echoed. Visions of the pair's first secret meeting danced through her head. This new connection between Lynsey and Malory was suspicious. It was weird enough for Lynsey and Malory to talk together. But *ride* together? "Really, Malory? What's this about?"

Ali looked surprised at the blunt question. "Dylan, I'm not sure this is something that needs an explanation," she said. "My only concern is —" she stopped and glanced at Kelly who had just entered, interrupting her train of thought.

"The construction company's on the phone for you, Ms. Carmichael," Kelly said breathlessly. "They said it's important."

"All right, I'll be right there." Ali glanced at Lynsey and Malory. "I'll be right back, girls."

As soon as she was gone, Dylan turned to Malory. "What's going on here?" she demanded. "First you have a top secret conversation that you refuse to tell anyone about, and now you're going on a cozy little trail ride together? What's going on with you two? Are you, like, BFFs now?"

"Dylan . . ." Malory began.

"You don't have to answer her when she's being so rude," Lynsey broke in, glaring at Dylan. "It's none of her business what we do."

Dylan glared back. "Fine," she said. "Come to think of it, I'm in the mood for a trail ride myself. Maybe I'll join you."

"Oh, that would be good," Malory said before Lynsey could do more than sputter. "It would actually help us out. You know, Ms. Carmichael wasn't going to let us go unless we had a third, Lynsey. Barn rules. I'll go tell her we've got three riders now."

She darted out of the room before either of the others

could answer. There was a long moment of prickly silence, finally broken by Lynsey.

"Why do you have to poke your little pug nose into everyone else's business?" she demanded.

"Me?" Dylan let out a laugh of disbelief. "Are you insane? I'm not the one who's stealing friends and butting in where I don't belong."

"Yes, you so totally are." Lynsey rolled her eyes. "Surely you're not so clueless that you haven't realized the whole school's laughing at you and your counter petition. Do you really think it's your place to influence staffing decisions?"

"Oh, so my petition's stupid but Clare is right on with everything she's been doing, right?" Dylan shot back.

"I didn't say —"

"We're all set!" Malory said, bursting back into the room at that moment. "She said we could stay out for an hour or so, but we should keep away from the construction areas on the cross-country course."

"Just give me a second to tack up," Dylan said, although she wasn't feeling very enthusiastic about joining them for an impromptu trail ride. Was Lynsey right? Was everyone at Chestnut Hill laughing at her? And if so, why hadn't her friends told her?

She grabbed Morello's bridle off a hook on the wall and slung it over one shoulder. Then she gathered up his saddle, pad, and a stiff brush and rubber currycomb and raced to get her pony ready to ride.

She tacked up in record time, and within minutes the three girls were mounted and riding across the back field at a brisk walk. As soon as they'd passed the rings, the ponies figured out where they were headed, and all three of them perked up and quickened their pace. Tybalt seemed a bit nervous, prancing and snorting any time a leaf blew past or a bird chirped nearby, but, keeping one ear flicked back and listening to Malory as she spoke to him soothingly, he managed to stay calm.

"So," Dylan said after a few minutes passed in silence. "What's new?"

Lynsey turned in her saddle and glared at her. "Subtle," she pronounced sarcastically.

"What are you talking about? I'm just making conversation."

"Uh-huh." Lynsey let out a snort, which made Bluegrass's ear flick back toward her.

"I'm just saying, if there's anything in particular you guys had planned to talk about, don't let me stop you," Dylan said. "Just pretend I'm not here."

"Right. Sort of like you wanted us to pretend you weren't barging in on us in the dorm room the other night?" Lynsey said. "I don't know why you can't grasp the concept that some things just don't concern you. The Earth revolves around the sun, not Dylan Walsh."

"Oh, really!" Dylan exclaimed. "This coming from you of all people, the person who needs absolute silence to apply her makeup —"

"Stop it!" Malory cried, so loudly that Tybalt took a startled skip-step off to one side. "Can you both just quit it? This is ridiculous. Dylan, you're just going to have to take my word that this is *not* something you need to worry about, okay?"

Dylan was so surprised she couldn't speak for a second. Was Malory really going to insist on keeping Lynsey's secret?

Dylan looked at Lynsey. She had her usual irritated look on her face, but she also seemed to exude a sense of satisfaction. Her eyes were steely, and Dylan could swear her cheekbones somehow looked higher, giving her an even haughtier expression than usual.

"You're really not going to let me in on this?" she asked, giving Malory a questioning look.

Lynsey opened her mouth to respond, but Malory jumped in before she could get a word out. "Lynsey and I have been talking about something personal. There's really no reason for you to be concerned, Dylan. I'm sorry. If Lynsey wants to talk to you about it, that's up to her."

Lynsey shot Dylan a withering look that made it clear she was not going to be including Dylan on her little secret that day. The three girls rode on in silence for a while, and Dylan lost herself in thought. If they weren't going to tell her what was going on, fine. There was no reason she shouldn't try to enjoy this ride, even if there was clearly something strange going on with Malory and her newfound confidante.

The ponies had reached the edge of the woods. Turning to the right, the girls skirted the winter-bare tree trunks and spiky underbrush, heading toward one of the trails that wound through the forest and stretched all the way to the far western border of the expansive school grounds.

Lynsey's expression wavered between annoyed and hesitant. Finally she shrugged. "Okay," she said to Malory. "We're out on the trail like you wanted — now what?"

"This ride was your idea, Mal?" Dylan asked.

"My, my, aren't we full of questions today?" Lynsey said icily.

Malory answered more seriously.

"It was my idea because I thought the ponies could use a treat," she began, in an effort to answer both girls at once. "I think these guys do so much for us in the ring, they need some time to unwind. Tybalt has made real progress since he came to Chestnut Hill, but I don't want him to get overwhelmed, especially since we've been working so hard now. And Bluegrass is always so formal, I thought the change of scenery might help him to relax." As she added her thoughts on Bluegrass, Lynsey shot Malory a look that Dylan was sure had meaning, but she couldn't discern what that meaning might be. But Malory ignored Lynsey's pointed glare and kept on talking.

"It's amazing what a change of pace can do for the ponies. It can make them much more responsive in the ring." As she finished, Malory leaned over and gave Tybalt a heartfelt rub on the neck.

Dylan was always amazed by Malory's ability to understand what the ponies needed. Tybalt couldn't have ended up in better hands, and Dylan was sure Malory would always follow the right path in getting Tybalt to adjust to his life at Chestnut Hill — her instincts were never wrong when it came to her pony. What Dylan couldn't understand was why Malory was suddenly investing her energy in Lynsey and Bluegrass. It wasn't as if Bluegrass ever missed out on any pony luxuries — Lynsey always made sure her pony had the best of everything. And it was strange that Lynsey would be taking suggestions from Malory on how to work with her horse in any case.

"Plus," Malory added, breaking into Dylan's thoughts, "everything seems different out here. It gives us a fresh take on things — and the ponies, too. Jumping logs out here is completely different than jumping fences in the ring."

"Logs?" Lynsey repeated, sounding wary. "I don't know about that. If Bluegrass hurts himself . . ."

Dylan rolled her eyes. Ever since she'd first heard

about the new cross-country course, Lynsey had been insisting that Bluegrass was much too valuable to go careening around the countryside jumping solid obstacles.

"Don't worry," Malory told Lynsey. "If Blue can jump a big oxer in the ring, he'll fly right over a one-foot-high log without a second thought."

Dylan couldn't help being impressed anew by her friend. She'd always respected the patient, sensitive way she approached her work with Tybalt. *And she has to be even more patient to deal with Lynsey!* she thought.

The three of them soon reached the trail that turned into the woods. After that, they stopped talking about riding and just chatted about nothing in particular as they walked and trotted along the smooth, winding trail.

If what Malory had said about the woods being relaxing for the ponies was right, it seemed to be even more true for Lynsey. The longer the three of them rode together, the more laid-back Lynsey seemed to get. She stopped shooting piercing glances at either Dylan or Malory and actually began to take part in conversations. She even made jokes and laughed at some of the things the other girls said about teachers and classes they were all struggling in. Dylan realized she was enjoying herself more than she had since spring break. She and Lynsey would never be friends, but she had to admit that her roommate was actually being tolerable for a change.

Maybe that's what happens when you get Lynsey out here in

the woods, away from the influence of her shallow, catty friends,
Dylan thought. *She's not really so obnoxious — it's just over-*
exposure to all that Dolce & Gabbana. . . .

Just then Lynsey glanced over at her. "What are you
smirking about?" she demanded. "You look like a mental patient."

"Takes one to know one," Dylan replied automatically. Then she burst out laughing, which just seemed to
agitate Lynsey further.

A few minutes later Dylan found herself and Morello
in the lead as they passed through a clearing and entered
a particularly wide, flat section of the trail. She noticed
that Malory and Lynsey were quietly exchanging some
words, now that she was out of earshot, but she tried not
to let it bother her. She knew she had to trust Malory.
"Come on," she called back to the others. "Should we try
a canter?"

Seconds later, all three ponies were flying along the
trail, their manes and tails whipping out behind them.
Morello tossed his head and snorted, clearly enjoying
himself. Dylan stayed in two-point position, her hands
buried in his fabulously warm mane.

They careened around a curve in the trail, Morello
automatically swapping leads. Straight ahead, Dylan
saw that a tree had fallen across the trail. The farside of
the trunk was resting on a rock, forming a barrier about
two feet tall.

It was too late to warn the others about the impending jump, and Morello had already fixed his attention on the obstacle, his ears pricked forward with determination and excitement. Dylan leaned forward as she prepared for the jump. Her spirit soared as they flew over the log without breaking stride.

"Whoo-hoo!" she cried when they landed. Sitting up, she slowed the pony and turned her head to watch as first Bluegrass and then Tybalt jumped the log just as easily.

Lynsey looked startled as she pulled her pony down to a trot along with the others. "Nice trail manners, Dylan," she exclaimed, sounding like her usual snooty self once more. "Did you ever hear of calling a heads-up? You could have gotten us all killed."

"Wow," Malory said before Dylan could answer. "Lynsey, Blue looked totally amazing jumping that log! He snapped his knees right up like a seasoned fox-hunter."

Lynsey's tense expression relaxed again into a self-satisfied smile. "Yes," she said. "Well, he didn't win a trunk full of trophies for jumping like a rhinoceros, you know."

In a short time, the trail doubled back on itself. The girls rode along on a loose rein; even Tybalt was strolling along like a laid-back trail horse. They were all enveloped in such a relaxed, friendly feeling that Dylan had to keep looking over to remind herself it was Lynsey Harrison riding along beside her.

Lynsey caught one of those glances. "Do you have a problem?" she demanded irritably. Without waiting for a response, Lynsey wrinkled her nose and proposed a new subject. "What's up with Ms. Carmichael lately?" she asked. "She's been pushing everyone so hard, like she's trying to prove something. Is she making a statement because she's worried that she's on her way out?"

"What?" Dylan exclaimed. "Don't tell me you bought into those stupid rumors, too?" She pretended to slap her forehead. "What am I saying? Of course you did — you're best friends with Patience the gossip queen, after all." She hoped Lynsey wouldn't realize that she was as concerned with the rumors as everyone else seemed to be.

"Patience is hardly the only one talking about it." Lynsey shot her a superior look. "Even someone as socially remedial as you must've heard what everyone's saying."

"What did Ali ever do to you?" Dylan shot back at her. "You sound like you'd love to see her kicked out so Ms. Mitchell can come back!"

Lynsey shrugged, leaning forward to flick away a leaf that had just landed in Bluegrass's mane. "There's no question that Ms. Mitchell got better results. My older sisters were both on the riding team when she was here. They always said she was the best coach they'd ever had."

"Well, they've never been coached by Ali. Just because

they're your sisters it doesn't mean they're right," Dylan exclaimed.

"And just because Ms. Carmichael is your aunt, doesn't mean she's the best person for the job," Lynsey replied smartly.

"Guys . . ." Malory spoke up, sounding uneasy.

But Dylan barely heard her. "Why don't you mind your own business?" she snapped at Lynsey.

"Look who's talking," Lynsey retorted. "I think I'll remind you of that remark the next time you try eavesdropping on my conversations and inviting yourself on trail rides."

"Guys!" Malory said, a little more loudly this time. "I think the ponies are bored. Let's trot!"

Without waiting for an answer, she nudged Tybalt forward. Dylan scowled at Lynsey one last time, then followed.

The whole ride back, Dylan stewed silently. Morello seemed to pick up on her change of mood; he started spooking every few minutes and did his best to yank the reins out of her hands for the rest of the ride. By the time they reached the stable area, the mood was positively glacial.

Dylan swung down from the saddle outside the barn. "I'll walk up to dinner with you after we put the ponies away," she told Malory, pointedly ignoring Lynsey, who had just dismounted nearby.

She led Morello inside and untacked him quickly in his stall. Then she grabbed the saddle and bridle and hurried toward the tack room to put them away.

Outside the tack room door she stopped short, recognizing Clare Houlder's voice coming from within. She was chuckling and thanking someone.

Dylan stepped through the door. Clare was just taking back a clipboard and pen from Kimberley Butler and Adriana Estevan, a pair of sophomores from the intermediate riding class. She saw Dylan and gave her a smile that looked more like a smirk. Then she turned back to the two sophomores.

"Thanks so much for signing, girls," she said. "With your help, maybe we'll have a winning team again soon." Her smile broadened as Lynsey stepped into the room holding Bluegrass's tack. "Lynsey! You're just the person I wanted to see!"

Dylan threw her saddle and bridle back on their racks. Then she raced out of the tack room and out of the barn, not even returning to Morello's stall to say good night. There was nothing she could do to stop her roommate from signing Clare's anti-Ali petition. She was kind of surprised that Ms. Harrison hadn't been one of the first to add her name. Still, Dylan wasn't about to hang around and watch Lynsey pen her smug signature on the list.

CHAPTER TWELVE

Dylan awoke early on Saturday morning. For once her first thought wasn't of the whole Ali situation. She smiled and glanced over at the lump under the covers in the bed across the room.

"Rise and shine, Felicity Harper," she sang out, hopping out of bed and hurrying over to poke Honey between the shoulder blades.

At first Honey merely moaned, hugging her pillow and nestling farther under her blankets. Dylan waited for a second — sometimes it took Honey a few tries to wake up.

"Hey," she said when Honey went still again. "Out of bed already. You don't want to keep Minnie waiting, do you?"

At that, Honey's eyes flew open and she sat up. "Oh!" she said, suddenly wide awake. "Is it finally Saturday?"

"Yup." Dylan stepped over to her chest of drawers and

grabbed a clean pair of jeans. "Now hurry up and get dressed. The sooner we finish breakfast, the sooner we can get down to the barn to make sure Minnie is ready to go."

The past couple of days had passed quickly, and Dylan was trying not to feel guilty about not doing more to help her aunt. She and Lani had made plans to collect signatures on their petition before and after classes each day, but somehow their plans always fell through. On Thursday morning, Lani had overslept, and that afternoon there had been a yearbook meeting that ran longer than usual. Friday morning, Dylan had to make up a test that she missed when she was sick. And on Friday afternoon, the girls' good intentions were thwarted by an emergency outfit consultation for the Spring Fling. Of course, Lynsey's comments about other students mocking the counter petition had also dampened Dylan's enthusiasm for her plan. But the best excuse for putting off the petition was to support Honey.

Before long, Dylan, Lani, and Malory were in the barn busily brushing Minnie's coat to a sheen while Honey hovered nearby fiddling with her helmet strap. The pretty gray mare stood relaxed in the cross-ties with one hind leg cocked, her soft eyes focused on Honey.

"Ready to get started, Honey?" Ms. Carmichael asked, as she walked down the aisle toward them. "I see you've brought your own cheering section along."

Dylan smiled. "What can we say? We're her biggest fans."

"Yeah," Lani quipped, giving Minnie a pat. "And Honey's not bad, either."

Ms. Carmichael smiled. "Well, it's nice to see you girls acting like a team."

Dylan could tell that Honey was still feeling nervous as she bridled Minnie and led her outside a few minutes later. "You can do it," Dylan whispered to Honey, giving her arm a squeeze.

"I hope so," Honey replied. "I've been dying to ride Minnie for so long. But now that it's time, I just keep thinking about all the problems Patience had with her. . . ."

"Don't think about that," Dylan said. "Patience knows about as much about horses as I know about the stock market. You're way better than her. Plus you've been spending so much time with Minnie these past couple of months that you probably know her better than anyone. You're going to do great!"

"Let's go to the indoor ring," Ms. Carmichael said, stepping out of the barn. "It's a little breezy today, and we don't want any distractions."

"Minnie's so solid she probably never gets distracted," Dylan murmured to Lani. "But I'm not so sure about Honey."

Lani grinned. "If you think she's shaky now, wait till

you see her tonight — right before her first slow dance with Josh."

Honey overheard the last part and shot Lani and Dylan a disgruntled look. Dylan burst out laughing as Lani glanced skyward and whistled innocently. Malory's attention was focused on the pony.

As Honey checked her girth and then mounted, Dylan crossed her fingers on her friend's behalf. She knew how much Honey had been looking forward to this moment.

But it didn't look like Honey and Minnie were going to need any extra luck. From the second they stepped off from the mounting block, the two hardly made a wrong move. It was clear to everyone watching that Honey had learned a lot since the beginning of the year, when she almost didn't make it into the intermediate class. Now she was able to put the well-trained pony through her paces as if they'd been working together for months.

"Wow, she's doing great," Dylan commented to Malory and Lani.

Malory nodded. "Before she came here, she'd only ridden one or two ponies besides her own," she said. "Since the beginning of the year, she's ridden so many different ponies, she's good at figuring out a new horse and adjusting her signs."

"Plus Minnie's probably relieved not to have Patience up there kicking her in the gut," Lani added. It sounded like Lani's typical brand of humor, but Dylan was sure there was substantial truth in it.

"Want to try a jump?" Ali called to Honey, who had just finished a couple of canter circles.

Honey nodded, then bit her lip. "Is that okay?" she said. "Her tendons . . . I don't want to . . ."

"We'll keep it small," Ali said. "I just want to see how she does, if you feel up to it."

Honey glanced over at her friends, took a deep breath, and then nodded and smiled. Dylan gave her a thumbs-up.

Soon Ms. Carmichael had set up a cross rail. "Just trot up to it, nice and easy," she called. "Eyes forward, heels down . . ."

Honey circled Minnie and then pushed her into a trot. The mare's fuzzy gray ears pricked forward as she saw the fence, but her gait remained steady and even. When she reached the cross rail, she arced over it neatly and cantered a few steps away on the other side.

As she pulled up, Honey was grinning from ear to ear. "That felt great!"

"It looked great, too." Ms. Carmichael smiled back. "Want to try it once more from a canter?"

After a few more jumps over the cross rail, Ali brought the lesson to an end. Honey walked Minnie for a few minutes to cool her down — unlike most of the school ponies, the pretty gray mare hadn't been clipped since before her injury, so it was important to make sure she cooled down enough for her coat to dry before going back outside. Dylan, Malory, and Lani joined her in the arena, walking beside the pony so they could talk to Honey.

"Hey, we'd better be careful," Dylan joked after a few minutes of walking. "We don't want to wear ourselves out before tonight, or we'll be too tired to get down on the dance floor."

"Don't think of it as tiring ourselves out," Lani advised. "Think of it as warming up."

"Yeah, we wouldn't let our ponies jump a course without a warm-up," Malory said. "We shouldn't let ourselves dance without one, either. Otherwise we might strain our tendons."

Dylan nodded somberly. "Or pull a stifle. Or maybe damage our hocks."

"The way you dance, Dylan, I wouldn't be at all surprised," Honey said with a grin.

Lani laughed. "Are you kidding? The way *she* dances, I think *our* hocks might be in more danger than her own!"

Dylan gave her friend a horrified look as she pretended to be insulted. It felt good for all four of them to be together. As they brought Minnie back into the barn, Dylan thought how things felt almost normal — when she didn't fixate on it, her frustration with Malory's new-found friendship with Lynsey seemed nonexistent.

Come to think of it, Dylan realized, *Aunt Ali seemed like her old self today, too.* She had been fabulously supportive of Honey, not pushing her as she'd been doing to all the students in riding class lately.

When the girls arrived at Minnie's stall, they found Kelly inside, spreading fresh straw on the ground.

"Hey, guys," Kelly said, resting on the pitchfork handle. "Minnie can go out once she's untacked, if you want to drop her off for me."

"Sure!" Honey said. "Which pasture?"

Soon the four friends were leading Minnie up a hilly path toward Chestnut Hill's second-largest pasture, which was serving as the mare pasture that week. As they neared the gate, which stood at the highest point on that part of campus, Dylan could see Foxy Lady, Sancha, Shamrock, Skylark, and several others grazing on the sparse grass, which was just beginning to show hints of spring green, or nibbling at one of the piles of hay scattered here and there throughout the ten-acre field.

She could also see something else. On an even higher rise beyond the pasture, a raw pile of reddish-brown dirt stood out like a wound against the grayish-green grass. *That's going to be the bank jump*, she thought with a flash of excitement, recalling the map of the proposed cross-country course that hung on the bulletin board in Aunt Ali's office.

"What are you looking at?" Lani asked, following Dylan's gaze. "Oh! Hey, check it out, guys! It looks like the course builders are back at work!"

Dylan shook her head. "Nope," she said, her mood plummeting as her thoughts returned to her aunt's escalating school problems. "That jump has been like that for weeks."

"Are you sure?" Malory asked. "I don't remember seeing it before."

"Positive," Dylan said. "When I had the flu, I helped turn out some horses up here, and I saw it then. Besides, I heard Kelly and Sara talking yesterday — the course is definitely still on hold."

"Oh, well." Honey shrugged. "We always knew the course wouldn't be finished until shortly before summer break, even without the delay. At least it should be ready and waiting for us when we return next autumn."

"Yeah," Dylan said with a sigh. "I just hope Aunt Ali will still be here to school us over it."

"We're here!" Lani sang out as she danced into the St. Kits ballroom. "It's time to get this party started!"

Dylan grinned as she followed Lani into the room. She was determined to forget her troubles for a while and have fun tonight. That new determination had started when all of Chestnut Hill had gone into a frenzy of party preparations that afternoon. Luckily, Lynsey had gone over to Patience's room to get ready, which meant Dylan and her friends had Room Two all to themselves. They'd turned Honey's desk into a makeup and hair station, and Dylan's bed had served as a wardrobe staging area. Dylan had dumped out her jewelry box onto her desk, encouraging her friends to borrow whatever they liked. Honey had some nice jewelry of her own — she'd chosen a pretty pearl necklace to go with her sky-blue empire-waisted dress — but Malory and Lani were decidedly lacking in the accessories department. As they got ready, various other friends from the dorm had stopped by to loan or borrow shoes, earrings, blush, stockings, lip gloss, and various other items.

By the time the four friends were ready to head downstairs to meet the fleet of Chestnut Hill vans scheduled to take them over to St. Kits, they all looked great. Malory's dress turned out to be just as fabulous on her as Dylan had pictured, and the addition of Dylan's best silver choker and a pair of Honey's Sigerson Morrison flats made her whole look even more perfect. Honey and Dylan had worked hard on Malory's hair, piling her dark hair loosely on top of her head and allowing a few soft curls to cascade around her face. All she'd needed after that was a touch of rose-tinted gloss on her lips and a little eyeliner and clear mascara to bring out the brilliance of her blue eyes.

"Whoa!" Dylan had said, stepping back to admire her handiwork after applying Malory's lip gloss. "Mal, you're a knockout! Caleb's going to have a stroke when he gets a load of you!"

"I hope not." Malory smiled bashfully. "Anyway, you look great, too, Dyl."

"You're absolutely right, if I do say so myself!" Dylan turned to admire herself in the full-length mirror on the back of the door. She was wearing a silk teal Marc Jacobs dress she'd bought in Aspen over the winter break, her favorite pair of Naughty Monkey sequined wedges, and a pair of funky Swarovski crystal earrings her mother had sent her from Amsterdam.

Honey looked fabulous, too. The pale blue of her dress complemented her soft coloring, and her blonde hair fell in a gleaming curtain to her shoulders.

Even cowgirl Lani was wearing a dress — a cute red halter dress she'd borrowed from her roommate Alexandra, who was just as tall as she was. With one of Dylan's chunky bracelets, a pair of clip-on hoop earrings borrowed from Razina down the hall, and her own silver ballet flats, she wouldn't have looked out of place in the pages of *Teen Vogue*.

With all the excitement and anticipation of the day, Dylan had succeeded in forgetting about her aunt's problems for a while. And now that they were at the dance, she expected to be far too busy keeping an eye on the budding romances of her friends to worry about anything else. In Dylan's opinion, both Malory and Honey could be horrendously reserved at times, and Dylan wanted to make sure they didn't let their shy personalities stand in the way of true love.

And if some irresistible St. Kits upperclassman sweeps me off my feet, I wouldn't turn him down, she thought as she glanced around at all the khaki-clad guys in the St. Kits ballroom. *After all, Henri hasn't exactly been e-mailing on a daily basis. And he may be unbearably cute — in that European sort of way — but he's also in France!* Dylan frowned as she realized she hadn't heard from Henri since her days in the Sick Suite even though she'd written to vent about the Ali situation. But she shrugged it off. Tonight there would be no worrying, only dancing. The St. Kits ballroom, like the rest of the school, looked like something out of a European castle. The dark paneled walls were draped with festive streamers in bright spring colors, and the oak floorboards had been polished to a mirror-like shine. Tables at one end of the cavernous room held large punch bowls and plenty of snacks. *Provisions,* Dylan thought. *Yum.*

Lani was looking around the room as well. "Okay, so where are the boyfriends?" she asked. "Shouldn't they have been waiting for Honey and Malory with flowers and stuff?"

"Shh!" Honey shushed her, her face flushing. "They aren't our boyfriends."

Dylan grinned at Lani. "Uh-oh, someone's blushing."

There was a commotion behind them as another vanload of Chestnut Hill students poured into the room. Among them were Lynsey and Patience. Both girls were even more dressed up than usual. Lynsey was lifting her feet extra-high with each step, apparently channeling her inner Clydesdale. Dylan deduced that she was trying to show off her new Giuseppe Zanotti beaded flats. Patience was wearing so much liner around her small, round eyes that she almost resembled a dramatic runway model. But Dylan didn't think she had pulled off the look. Instead the makeup seemed to say, "No really, I *do* have deep troubled thoughts, I swear!"

As Dylan was about to point out Patience's makeup madness to her friends, she saw Clare, Chloe, and Colette enter, along with a few of their non-riding junior friends. Dylan questioned Clare's choice of an animal-print skirt, but was distracted from this thought when she noticed that all of the girls were laughing and talking with unusual gusto.

Dylan frowned. Was it her imagination, or did Clare and her friends seem to be congratulating one another for something?

Colette is always a ditz, she thought. *And Chloe's probably just trying to make enough noise to get the boys to notice her. But*

Clare isn't usually so dramatic. Unless she's especially happy about something right now . . .

"Hey! Welcome to St. Kits."

Dylan turned to see Caleb and Josh approaching. Both boys looked handsome in button-down shirts and pressed khakis. Caleb was wearing loafers so highly polished they reflected the twinkling overhead lights, and Josh's blond hair, which usually fell haphazardly around his face, was slicked back with hair gel.

"Hey, guys," Dylan greeted them. "How's it going?"

Neither of them answered her, but she didn't mind. Caleb's mouth was agape as he stared at Malory, and Josh's cheeks were flushed as he smiled shyly at Honey.

"Wow," Caleb finally said, running one hand through his short dark hair. "Malory, you look — you look really different. I mean amazing!"

"Thanks." Malory glanced down and brushed an imaginary piece of lint off her skirt. "You look nice, too."

Josh nodded so vigorously that a chunk of hair escaped from the gel and flopped over his forehead. "Yeah, Honey," he blurted out, shoving the hair back into place without taking his eyes off her. "You look incredible." Suddenly seeming to notice Dylan and Lani standing there beaming at them, he added, "Um, you guys look good, too."

"Gee, thanks, Josh," Lani said. "Dylan and I picked out these outfits just for you."

The boys looked a little confused, but they smiled

good-naturedly. "Come on," Josh said, regaining his usual easygoing confidence. "I love this song. Do you want to dance?"

For the next hour or two, Dylan and her friends threw themselves into the fun, dancing in a group for the fast songs and then splitting off into pairs for the slow ones. At the sound of the chords of the first slow song, Lani playfully bowed to Dylan and asked her to dance. They swooped around the floor in a silly version of a tango. It wasn't long before a pair of St. Kits eighth-graders cut in and swept the two of them off to dance. After that, a steady stream of boys invited them onto the floor every time the music slowed.

"Who says being single is no fun?" Lani whispered to Dylan as yet another cute St. Kits boy led her off to dance.

After a while their little group was joined by Dylan's cousin Nat, who was a St. Kits freshman. Nat Carmichael was the type of person who was friends with everyone he met, and he introduced the girls to even more of his schoolmates. Dylan couldn't help noticing with amusement that anytime one of the new boys gave Malory an admiring look or comment, Caleb was quick to make an excuse to pull her away somewhere. Josh didn't seem quite as anxious about the attention Honey was getting, though he did have one hand on her arm or around her waist much of the time.

Finally, Dylan was ready to take a break. "I've got to

sit down," she told her friends breathlessly. "These shoes look fabulous, but they're killing my feet."

"I could use a rest, too," Honey admitted. She smiled at Josh. "Want to go and sit down?"

"Sure," Josh said as he brushed pieces of hair — which kept escaping from his gelled 'do — out of his face. "There's an empty bench over there."

"I'll catch you guys later," Nat said to them, waving to someone across the room. He took off into the crowd as Dylan, Lani, Honey, Malory, Josh, and Caleb headed toward one of the overstuffed velvet banquettes lining one wall.

Dylan found herself sitting between Caleb and Lani. "This is a blast," she commented to Caleb.

"Definitely," Malory agreed, leaning over from her spot on Caleb's other side. "You St. Kits guys really know how to throw a party."

"Well, we're just paying you back for the great All Schools show you threw for us," Caleb replied with a grin. "We really appreciated having such a nice setting to win all our ribbons."

"Boo, hiss!" Lani jeered as Honey, Dylan, and Josh laughed. "Talk about a sore winner."

Caleb grinned even more broadly. "Don't cry, you guys might win something one of these days," he joked. "Especially now that you'll have Elizabeth Mitchell back at Chestnut Hill."

Chapter Thirteen

Dylan sat frozen in shock for a split second. Then she reacted.

"What?" she shrieked in unison with Malory and Lani. The O shape of Honey's mouth matched the shocked expression in her eyes.

Caleb looked confused. He turned to Malory, whose face had gone pale with surprise. "Wait, isn't that old news?" he asked. "I heard someone from your school talking about it earlier when Josh and I went to get some punch."

"Who was it?" Dylan demanded.

Caleb shrugged, glancing over at Josh for help.

"I remember," Josh spoke up. "It was that blonde girl with the leopard-print skirt."

"Clare," Dylan said icily, searching the crowd. She couldn't see Clare or her friends at the moment, but she definitely remembered that skirt from when she'd first entered. "What did she say exactly?"

"I wasn't really paying attention," Caleb said. "But they were sure that Ms. Carmichael was going to resign, and Liz Mitchell would take up her old job as Director of Riding." His gaze fell on Dylan's shocked face, and he gulped. "Oh, sorry," he said. "I forgot she's your aunt. So you really didn't know?"

Dylan couldn't answer for a second. Her mind was racing. Had Clare found out some new information? Was that why she'd looked so smug coming into the dance?

"There have been a few rumors," Honey said. "But we never thought there was anything to them." She shot Dylan a slightly guilty look. "Well, *most* of us didn't, anyway."

"Yeah," Lani added. "I'm sure you must've heard wrong, Caleb. It was probably just Clare Houlder's wishful thinking or something."

"You could be right," Caleb said. "But you have to admit, the aunt thing aside, it wouldn't be all bad. Ms. Mitchell did have a great record at Chestnut Hill."

"What?" Malory stared at him in open horror. "How can you say that?"

"What do you mean?" Caleb seemed surprised by her reaction. "Chestnut Hill's riding teams won more titles under Ms. Mitchell than any other school in the league. Ms. Carmichael seems really friendly, but your show record so far this year, well . . . Anyone who was at that show two weeks ago knows it wasn't up to the Chestnut Hill standard. You guys usually dominate the league."

"Give her a chance," Honey protested. "Ms. Carmichael just got here this year. I'm sure it takes time to really hit your stride as a teacher."

"Sure." Caleb picked at a loose thread on the banquette seat. "I see your point. She might still step it up. But I'm just saying it wouldn't be a bad thing to have a proven winner coaching you."

"Okay, Mr. I-won-top-equitation-honors-at-the-last-show," Lani put in with a frown. "What you say makes sense, but competition aside, we happen to *like* Ms. Carmichael. We don't want her to leave, no matter what kind of record she has."

Josh laughed, sounding a little uncomfortable. "Hey, Caleb is just making a point," he said, reaching over Malory's lap to smack Caleb on the knee. "I mean, I'm not a rider, but I know sports, and I know having a coach who can win is key."

"Right." Malory's voice was so ice-cold that Dylan glanced over at her in surprise. "*If* you think winning shows is the only important part of a riding program."

Caleb smiled uncertainly at her. "Maybe not the *only* important part," he said. "But you have to admit it's probably the *most* important part."

"No. I don't have to admit that," Malory said. "I

happen to believe the relationships and understanding we have with the horses are what's most important. And Ms. Carmichael's very supportive of that — no matter what. If it hadn't been for her, there's no way Tybalt would still be at Chestnut Hill." Malory swallowed, and she seemed to be deep in thought. "Ms. Carmichael is helping me learn the Heartland methods," she went on. "Those methods kept Tybalt here, and they're working really well on Blue —" she stopped glancing around guiltily. She finished by adding, "Winning shows is a long way from being the most important part of riding."

Dylan winced. Suddenly she realized what had been going on between Malory and Lynsey — Lynsey had been asking for help. She hadn't been playing along with Clare and her cronies by faking her mistakes in the ring. Bluegrass had been having some real setbacks lately. Now that Dylan thought about it, doing anything intentionally to make herself look bad was decidedly not Lynsey's style. Her whole life was about looking good. And of course she wouldn't want anyone to know Bluegrass was having problems. Dylan felt like her chest had collapsed. She couldn't believe she'd ever doubted Malory's motives for talking to Lynsey.

Bringing her attention back to the scene in front of her, Dylan shuddered. Malory didn't just seem distant now — she sounded downright angry. *Not that I blame her*, Dylan thought. *Caleb's acting like a total meathead.*

"But Mal," Caleb protested, sounding puzzled. "I don't get it. The shows *are* important. How else are you going to figure out how well your program is working?" He glanced over at Josh for support. "That would be like saying you don't care if your basketball team wins. It just doesn't make sense."

"Maybe not to you." Malory folded her arms over her chest.

"Try to understand," Honey put in earnestly. "We love riding with Ms. Carmichael. We learn more from her than how to impress judges. That means more to us than winning."

"Not that we don't want to win," Dylan put in. "We do. And we will. We just had a bad day at that last show. It could happen to anyone."

"Sure." Josh leaned back against the banquette's tall back, his blond hair standing out against the dark velvet. He glanced at Caleb. "Anyway, dude, there *are* other reasons for playing basketball. It's fun, for one thing. It's good exercise. Stuff like that."

"I guess." Caleb didn't sound convinced. "But it doesn't really matter one way or the other for you guys. It sounds like Ms. Mitchell is coming back, no matter what we all think." He grinned at Josh. "With Ms. Mitchell back in charge, I'll have to practice even harder to beat these guys at the next All Schools show."

Josh laughed. But he froze when Malory stood up, glared at both him and Caleb, and disappeared into the crowd.

"Yikes," Caleb said, staring after her. "What'd I say?"

Dylan scowled at him. "Are you kidding? If you really don't know, I can't help you." She got up and hurried after Malory, with Lani and Honey right behind her.

They found Malory in the vast, portrait-lined lobby area outside the ballroom. The bass from the music on the dance floor was still pounding away but the lack of people gave the room a desolate feeling. Malory was slumped in a chair near the front door, her face in her hands. When Dylan approached and said her name, Malory lifted her head. Even in the dim light coming from the antique chandelier overhead, Dylan could see that she was distraught.

"Hey, Mal." Dylan dropped to her knees and put an arm around her friend's shoulders.

Malory shook her head. She didn't say anything, but the look on her face spoke volumes.

Dylan didn't know what to say. Her head was spinning with everything that had just happened. First the news that Ali might really be leaving, then the fact that Malory had put her differences with Lynsey aside to help Bluegrass, and finally the discovery that Caleb was some kind of hypercompetitive freak who only cared about winning. As she gazed into Malory's eyes, the pain she saw there was heartbreaking. So much for the perfect couple . . .

☙

"Dylan, there you are." Nat casually made his way to Dylan, who was standing with her friends outside the women's restroom in the lobby. It was almost eleven o'clock, which meant the Chestnut Hill vans would be there any moment now to take the girls back to their dorms. "I've been looking for you guys all night. Where'd you run off to?"

Dylan shot a glance at Malory, who was still red-eyed and solemn. "Um, we just — we were sort of — around. I guess we just missed each other."

She wished she could tell him what Caleb had said, but that was out of the question. Ali was Nat's mother — if the rumor about Ali leaving her job were true, it would have an even bigger effect on his life than on any of theirs.

Nat looked perplexed, but he seemed to understand that it wasn't the best time to ask questions. "Well, okay," he said. "I heard your vans are here, so I wanted to come say good-bye."

Dylan felt guilty for keeping secrets from her cousin. But she didn't know what else to do. She couldn't exactly tell him that she and her friends had been hiding in the women's room for the past hour. They'd gone there after Caleb had tracked them down in the lobby wanting to speak to Malory. She had been too upset and angry to talk to him, so she'd headed into the bathroom to wash her face. Her friends had gone with her. No one had felt like dancing anymore, and they all wanted to avoid trying to explain the situation to Caleb. He still didn't have a clue about what he had said.

Realizing that Nat was still standing there looking at her, Dylan grabbed him in a big hug. "I'll talk to you soon," she murmured into the fabric of his long-sleeved polo shirt.

A few older boys standing nearby started to whoop and holler at the embrace. Nat hugged Dylan back, shooting them a dirty look. "Lay off, losers," he called. "She's my cousin, okay?"

Dylan smiled sadly, keeping her arms wrapped around him for a few seconds longer. She would really miss Nat if he and Aunt Ali moved back to Kentucky. He was the closest thing she'd ever had to a big brother.

"Bye," she said as he pulled away, looking a little embarrassed.

She followed her friends, who were already heading outside. Malory seemed particularly in a rush to get on the van and back to Chestnut Hill. Dylan couldn't blame her.

Heading outside, Dylan saw her three friends lined up

to get into one of the vans. The driver, a ruddy-faced man she recognized as one of the school custodians, was just opening the sliding side door.

"Wait, you guys! Hey, Honey, wait up!" Josh emerged from the building and jogged toward them from the entrance. He'd left his coat inside and had his arms wrapped around himself against the chilly night air. His hair had totally escaped the bonds of the gel now, and it fell into his eyes, giving him his usual casual charm.

"Oh, hi." Honey sounded tentative as she greeted him. "What is it, Josh? We really need to get going."

"I was just wondering if you were planning to go into Cheney Falls next Saturday," Josh said uncertainly, glancing from one somber girl's face to the next before returning his attention to Honey. "If you are, I thought maybe we could meet up. What do you think?"

Honey hesitated. She glanced at Malory, who was staring off into space with a bleak expression on her face. "I — I don't think so, Josh," Honey said. "I'm sorry."

Dylan closed her eyes, feeling horrible. Why was everything going so wrong all of a sudden? It was as if those first obnoxious comments of Clare's at the horse show had grown and spread, poisoning everyone and everything, like a virus of bad luck running through Chestnut Hill. Now, not only had Malory's romance been ruined, but Honey's appeared to be in danger, too.

"Come on, guys," Lani called. "We need to go."

When Dylan climbed inside the van, Lani was already sitting in the backseat. She flopped down beside her, suddenly feeling exhausted. Malory and Honey squeezed in on Dylan's other side.

Malory glanced over at Honey. "You could have agreed to meet up with him," she said. "I wouldn't mind."

"No." Honey shook her head. "It's okay."

After that, all four of them fell into a gloomy silence. A gaggle of Meyer and Walker eighth-graders climbed aboard and took the front two rows of seats, chattering excitedly to one another about the dance. After a curious glance or two into the rear seat, they seemed to forget that Dylan and her friends were back there at all.

As the van bounced along the dark, winding country roads, all Dylan could do was stare out the window and try not to think about anything.

CHAPTER FOURTEEN

Dylan's brain swam into consciousness at the sound of giggling. Her whole body felt heavy and warm, with that feeling she only got when she'd slept for a long time.

I guess the nurse was right about not being back to normal yet. That busy post-flu week kicked my butt, she thought woozily. *I must have really needed to sleep.*

Opening one eye, she squinted in the midday sunlight beaming through the big window at the end of the room. Lynsey and Patience were standing near Lynsey's bed. The two girls had just had Sunday brunch with Patience's mom, and they had obviously dressed in their Sunday best — Lynsey was just shrugging off her Rebecca Taylor faux-fur coat, and Patience was still wearing her chocolate-brown Twill Twenty Two jacket with a hat to match. Honey was nowhere in sight but her bed was neatly made, with her stuffed bear, Woozle, in his usual spot on her pillow.

How late had she slept? Turning her head, Dylan saw from the clock on her bedside table that it was a few minutes after noon. *Thank goodness for lazy Sunday mornings,* she thought with a contented sigh.

Stifling a yawn, she rubbed her eyes and sat up. Lynsey and Patience turned to look at her.

"It's alive," Lynsey said dryly. She kicked off her Moschino flats and grabbed her custom paddock boots from under her bed.

Patience smirked. "I can't believe you actually slept through brunch. Don't you have some animal instinct that prevents you from ever missing a chance to eat?" she chided Dylan.

"Whatever." Dylan yawned again as she swung her legs over the edge of the bed. It was chilly in the room, so she grabbed a pair of sweatpants from the floor next to her bed and pulled them on under her nightgown before she stood up and slid into her slippers.

Patience leaned over and whispered something to Lynsey, but Dylan was still too groggy to care. Figuring a shower would wake her up, she walked over to her dresser and pulled out a clean towel.

"I was so glad today to hear about my mom's discussion with Dr. Starling. It really is time they made some serious changes in the riding program. And I guess you wouldn't have time to eat brunch today, anyway," Patience said, turning to Dylan with a laugh. "You probably want to get down to the stable to help Ms. Carmichael finish packing up. I was just there, and it looks like she's got her truck almost ready to go."

That cut through the fog in Dylan's brain. "What?" she asked, turning to stare at Patience. "What did you say about Ms. Carmichael?"

Patience pursed her lips and shot Lynsey an amused glance. "Didn't you hear?" she asked innocently. "Your aunt has been packing up to leave campus all morning. I was just down at the stable delivering a message to Dr. Starling — she was there, too, of course — and . . ."

Dylan didn't wait to hear anymore. Could it be true? Was Aunt Ali planning to quit her position to avoid the humiliation of being asked to leave? "No, she can't — I've got to get down there!"

"Nice, Patience," Lynsey said sarcastically, glancing up from lacing up her paddock boots. "Listen, Dylan . . ."

"No!" Dylan cried. "I don't have time to listen to you gloat right now." Grabbing her favorite Juicy Couture hoodie from the pile of dirty clothes in front of her wardrobe, she yanked it on over her nightshirt. Then she kicked off her slippers and shoved her bare feet into a pair of moccasins sitting by her bed.

"But Dylan!" Lynsey's voice rose. "You really need to —"

"No, Lyns," Patience interrupted, cutting her off. "You heard her. She doesn't want to hear what you have to say."

Casting one last glance at Patience's gleeful face, Dylan grabbed the pro-Ali petition off her desk, and Honey's barn jacket off the hook by the door and ran out of the room. Some people might be happy that Ali was packing up to leave Chestnut Hill. But Dylan was going to do whatever she could to make sure it didn't happen.

"Hey, Dylan, wait!" Lynsey called after her. But Dylan ignored her.

If I show Aunt Ali the petition, she thought frantically as she raced down the stairs two at a time, *maybe it will convince her that it's worth fighting for her job. It might not have any effect on Dr. Starling's decision, but Ali might try harder to stay.*

She flew through the lobby, ignoring the startled looks from several of her dorm mates at the sight of her striped nightshirt under her jacket. One of them, a sophomore named Polly Cooke, called out her name as she raced past, but Dylan was too busy worrying about getting to Ali to answer, let alone slow her pace.

Outside, she left the path in favor of a shortcut across the grass. Clutching the petition in her hand, she ran as fast as she could toward the stable area.

Why did I have to sleep so late today of all days? Dylan wondered helplessly as she skidded around a horse trailer someone had left parked at the head of the stable driveway.

She stopped and glanced around the stable yard. A couple of school ponies were dozing in the sunshine in one of the dirt paddocks close to the barn, but all the outdoor rings were empty at the moment. There was no sign of her aunt or Dr. Starling anywhere. Hurrying to check the main barn, she stuck her head in and saw Kelly inside sweeping the aisle.

"Where's Al — um, Ms. Carmichael?" she called, trying to keep the anxiety out of her voice.

Kelly glanced up from her work. "Hasn't she left yet?" she asked. "I haven't seen her in a while."

Dylan's stomach clenched. So it was true. . . .

She darted back out of the barn. A quick glance assured her that Ali's pickup was still parked in its usual spot. Whew! So she *hadn't* left yet.

She dashed across the yard to the second barn, and headed straight for the office. As Dylan ran into the courtyard, several horses hung their heads out over their Dutch doors to watch, including one familiar dappled gray mare.

"Quince!" Dylan breathed, her gaze settling on the long nose of her aunt's horse. "You're still here!"

But she knew the fact that Aunt Ali hadn't gotten her horses ready to travel didn't necessarily mean anything. Even if she was planning to resign and move out immediately, she might have asked to leave her two horses at Chestnut Hill for a few more days until shipping arrangements could be made. She raced on to the stable office. But it was dark and empty.

Now what? Dylan clenched her fists around her petition, wondering what to do next. While she was thinking, she looked down at the petition in her hands. *How could I have passed up so many chances to get signatures?* she berated herself. *Will this really be enough to make a difference?*

"Dr. Starling!" she cried. If her aunt wasn't at the barn, maybe she was up at the school office giving her official resignation. There might still be time to stop her!

Dylan took off back around the stable block, aiming for the driveway that led up the hill toward the Old House. But the sound of voices from nearby stopped her in her tracks.

"Aunt Ali?" she called out tentatively.

She rounded the back of the main stable building and spotted her aunt standing with Sara Chappell in one of the small private paddocks that opened off the back row of stalls. Mischief Maker was tied to the fence, his head lowered and his eyes half closed as the two humans peered at his feet.

"Ali!" Dylan cried, racing over. "Thank goodness I caught you!"

Ali looked up with a smile. "Oh, hi, Dylan," she said, sounding as relaxed and normal as ever. She blinked as she took in the tail of Dylan's nightgown hanging down over her sweatpants. "You'll be glad to hear that ol' Mischief here is doing much better." She gave the big bay gelding a pat on the shoulder. "He's sound on that foot again already."

Sara nodded, her eyes sparkling with relief. "But I'm still going to keep him out of the next couple of shows, just to be safe," she told Ali. "Okay?"

Dylan was unable to contain herself any longer. Aunt Ali, can we go to your office for a second? I really need to talk to you."

Ali looked surprised, but she shrugged agreeably. "Sure. Sara, it's fine with me if you want to be cautious about reintroducing Mischief to the ring. We can talk more about how you want to handle things later."

Leaving Sara and Mischief behind, Dylan and Ali crossed the stable yard in silence. Once they were both in the office, Ali leaned against the edge of the desk, resting her hands beside her.

"What's going on, Dylan?" she asked. "It must be awfully serious if you ran down here half-dressed. I've heard the fashion police on campus can be brutal if they catch you like that."

Dylan didn't even crack a smile. Taking a deep breath, she held out her petitions. "It *is* serious," she said. "I came to give you this."

Ali took the paper and glanced at it. "'We the undersigned members of the Chestnut Hill community believe Ms. Ali Carmichael to be an outstanding Director of Riding . . .'" she began. Her brow furrowed momentarily, and then she set the petition aside. "Dylan, you didn't have to do this."

Before Dylan knew what was happening, her aunt had enveloped her in a big bear hug. Dylan hugged her back in surprise.

"What was that for?" she asked when Ali pulled away.

"For being such a loyal niece — and riding student," Ali said. "I really appreciate that you did this, Dylan." She waved one hand to indicate the petition.

Dylan's brain was spinning. She wondered if it was possible that she was still asleep and dreaming this whole scene, because it wasn't unfolding at all as she'd expected. How could Ali sit there looking so relaxed when her whole career was in jeopardy?

"I don't think you understand. I did the petition because Clare Houlder and some of her friends —"

Her aunt held up a hand to stop her. "I know about all that," she said. "Clare and Chloe turned their petition in to the school office yesterday afternoon."

"Oh." Dylan grimaced. She thought back to the Three C's apparent glee at the dance the night before and put two and two together.

"Dr. Starling stopped by this morning to give me a heads-up," Ali said. "She wanted me to know that there was dissension in the ranks, even though only a couple dozen students signed Clare's petition."

"A couple dozen?" Dylan was astonished. "That's all

they got? My petition has almost one hundred — see?" She reached forward and put the petition in front of her aunt again.

But Ali waved it away. "It's okay — I'm really not interested in seeing who signed or who didn't," she said. "I'm already aware of who the ringleaders are, and I'll be having a talk with them about their concerns."

"It's not just the petition, you know," Dylan blurted out. "Clare and her friends —"

"You mean their theatrics the other day?" Ali asked, raising her eyebrows. "I'm not quite as clueless as you think I am, Dylan. I saw what they were up to. I know the grid was a little more challenging than usual. But since when do Kingfisher and Hardy have so much trouble regulating their own strides?" she paused, letting her words sink in. "It's frustrating that those students found it necessary to stage such a thing, but I hope I'll gain their respect in time. It has more to do with them than me, I think.

Dylan's jaw dropped. "So you knew about that, too? But weren't you worried about what might happen if people started to talk?"

"Not really. I'm confident that I'm doing the job Dr. Starling wants me to do, and that most people are smart enough to recognize that. Dr. Starling is satisfied with my performance, and she's the only one responsible for making staff decisions — not a few cranky students." Ali smiled.

Dylan's mind raced as she tried to put all the pieces together. "But what about Ms. Mitchell coming here to see Dr. Starling? Didn't that worry you? I mean, everyone thought she was coming to ask for her job back."

Ali went on to explain that Ms. Mitchell and Dr. Starling were working together to organize a joint symposium with members of the U.S. Eventing Team. The idea was to have top international riders give classes on a variety of topics and to put more emphasis on eventing in the riding programs of both Chestnut Hill and Allbrights in the near future.

"Wow. That sounds cool," Dylan said, though she was still feeling a little stunned by all these revelations. Then something else occured to her. "Wait, so why were you so tough on all the riding classes this past few weeks? I figured you wanted to prove you could do the job and be as tough as Ms. Mitchell."

"Not even close. Come on, Dylan — can't you guess what that was about? What's my favorite word around the barn?"

Dylan blinked. "Uh — heels down?" she guessed. "No wait, that's two words. . . ."

"No Dylan," Ali said with a warm smile. "It's *team-work*. I was disappointed in our performance at the last show, but not because of our final score. It was because I heard a lot of *I* instead of *we*. One of the things I've been hoping to instill in you girls is the importance of working together to solve your issues. I thought by pushing you a bit more in class it might help you band together and achieve that sense of camaraderie."

"Oh." Dylan nodded slowly. "I think I get it."

"Yes, I know you do." Ali smiled at her. "You and your friends already have the concept of teamwork down pretty well most of the time. I'm proud of you guys for that. I only wish some of your attitude would rub off on a few of the other students at Chestnut Hill." She reached out to give Dylan another warm hug. "I'm sorry you were so worried, Dylan," she added. "But thank you so much for your efforts to save my job, even if things weren't as desperate as they seemed. I love being at Chestnut Hill — I can't imagine a more rewarding job and I'm not going anywhere."

Dylan was glad to hear it, but there was still one last worry nagging at the back of her mind. As Ali released her from the hug, she cleared her throat. "But a lot of people still think the team should've ridden better this last time. And that it was unfair for us to have to compete right after we got back from break, especially with that new wall jump. . . ."

Ali leaned back on the desk. "The scheduling issue was unfortunate. But the horses were plenty fit enough, which means it was mostly just a mental game for the riders. That goes double for the wall. Anyone who went into the show ring thinking she was at a disadvantage probably was. And anyone who was afraid her horse might not want to jump the wall was practically asking for a spook or a refusal." She shook her head ruefully. "Don't worry, we'll be working on those issues for the rest of the semester, too."

"Hmm." Dylan thought about what her aunt was saying for a second. Maybe Ali was right. After all, Malory and several others had done well even though everyone had been in the same situation. And once Dylan had recovered from her momentary nerves about the wall, Morello had jumped it just fine.

"If nothing else, that show was a valuable learning experience," Ali said. "Team spirit isn't just about riding. It's about being loyal to your teammates, and supporting one another through bad luck and bad riding as well as when things go well."

Dylan's mind flashed to Clare Houlder. *After hearing the way Clare talked about Kelsey behind her back at the show, I'm not surprised Ali doesn't want her on the team*, she thought.

"I see your point," she told her aunt.

"Good," Ali said. "So is there anything else? I was on my way out. . . ."

"Yeah, about that," Dylan said, remembering her earlier panic. "Where the heck are you going to on a Sunday morning? When Patience told me you were packing up your truck, and Kelly said she thought you'd already left, I practically had a heart attack!"

Ali laughed. "Oh, Dylan," she said. "This school can be like one big game of Telephone sometimes! I was getting ready to take the school's truck and trailer to a farm out in Page County to look at a couple of horses." She winked. "But don't worry, I'll be back by four. The foreman of the construction company is stopping by then."

"Really?" Dylan said. "Does that mean . . . ?"

"Our course is back on track." Ali nodded. "They hired on some more help so they can continue with our project while they work on the emergency one at the same time."

"Yes!" Dylan's face lit up. "I can't wait to tell the others — they're going to be so psyched!"

Dylan said good-bye and hurried out of the office, suddenly aware of the beautiful early spring day all around her. She also became all too aware of her less-than-perfectly-groomed appearance. It was no big deal to tuck her nightgown up out of sight under Honey's jacket, but if her hair looked anything like it usually did first thing in the morning, she knew there would be no hiding the fact that she'd just rolled out of bed. For once she was wholeheartedly glad that there were no boys at Chestnut Hill!

Oh well, she thought, turning toward the main stable building. A burst of familiar laughter and talking escaped from the building, and Dylan decided to see if her friends had come down while she was in Ali's office. *If I see any yearbook photographers lurking around, I'll just have to duck.*

She hurried into the barn, bursting with her good news. Her three best friends were nowhere in sight, but when she saw Lynsey at Bluegrass's stall, Dylan couldn't resist confronting her.

"Well, you'll be sorry to hear what Ali just told me," Dylan said.

Lynsey looked her up and down. "What's that?" she inquired. "That she's just passed a rule prohibiting all riders from wearing socks?"

Dylan glanced down at her own bare ankles. "No," she said, not bothering to dignify Lynsey's lame joke with any further response. "She told me she's staying at Chestnut Hill. Clare's stupid little petition didn't work."

"Why *would* Clare's petition work?" Lynsey replied with a raised eyebrow. "Whatever brain malfunction made you think it was okay to go out in public looking like that must be pretty bad. I don't know why either of you thought you'd be able to influence staffing decisions."

"Then maybe you'd like to explain to me why you signed Clare Houlder's petition against Ms. Carmichael?"

Lynsey looked surprised. "Oh, please," she exclaimed. "I didn't sign that thing — hardly anybody did. When

Colette was pestering me with it yesterday, she only had, like, twenty signatures. And most of them weren't even riders, let alone team members." She shrugged. "As far as I saw, nobody on the senior team signed at all."

"Really?" Dylan's mood, already buoyant after her chat with her aunt, soared even higher. For once, Lynsey's haughty expression wasn't even setting her nerves on edge — at least not too much.

"Whatever." Lynsey sounded disinterested. "It wouldn't make sense for me to sign, since I didn't have any direct experience with Ms. Mitchell's training." She flicked a hay speck off her Raven hipsters. "My older sisters were coached by Ms. Mitchell and she always said that you're only as good as your last show results. If Ms. Carmichael believed that, too, Blue and I would be off the team by now."

Dylan was so stunned that she couldn't answer. It was all she could do to keep her jaw from dropping so far open so she wouldn't drool on Honey's jacket.

Lynsey turned to let herself into her pony's stall. "And by the way, I was trying to tell you Patience was just messing with you," she added over her shoulder. "But I guess parading around campus in that outfit was too important for you to stop and listen to what I was saying."

"Oh." Dylan blushed, remembering how easily she'd fallen for Patience's trick. She also suddenly recalled

Lynsey trying to stop her from rushing out of the room. "Oh. Yeah," she mumbled. "Well, I guess I'll see you later."

"Dylan! There you are," Lani called, walking into the barn at that moment with Honey and Malory right behind her. "We thought you'd been abducted by aliens or something."

"I told them how you were out like a log when I left for brunch," Honey said. "We were just talking about going on a trail ride — Ms. Carmichael already said it's okay — but we didn't want to go until we found you. And here you are!"

"A trail ride sounds great," Dylan said. "But first, I have some big news. Aunt Ali is definitely staying!" She outlined what her aunt had just told her.

"That's awesome!" Lani exclaimed. "After last night, I was actually worried. In fact, I was feeling kind of guilty about not believing you before, Dyl."

"Me, too." Honey smiled. "But this is brilliant news!"

"I know." Dylan smiled back. "And if Clare and her friends don't like it, too bad. The rest of the school knows Ali's the best."

"She really is an amazing teacher," Malory said more seriously. "She just wants everyone to do their best. And another Riding Director wouldn't have given a pony like Tybalt a chance."

Honey nodded. "Or kept Minnie around long enough

to let her heal. Or let me ride her on her first time back to work."

"Plus, she comes across all friendly and easygoing, but she's pretty tough and disciplined underneath it all," Malory added. "I think that's one of the things that makes us all want to do well for her."

"Except for Dylan," Lani joked. "She just wants to kick butt at the shows."

"Very funny." Dylan stuck out her tongue. "Now come on, didn't you guys say something about a trail ride? Maybe we can ride over and check out the new cross-country course. Oh! I almost forgot . . ." She told them what Ali had said about the construction.

"This day just keeps getting better," Honey exclaimed. "Let's get out there and imagine we're already sailing over those fabulous coops and banks!"

"Works for me," Dylan said. She thought about running back to her dorm to change into more normal riding clothes, but decided against it. There were a few helmets and some spare pairs of old paddock boots in the tack room for the basic riders, and she was pretty sure she could find something to fit her. It wouldn't be the first time she'd ridden in sweats, though the nightgown would be a new touch. "Are all the ponies in?" she asked.

Honey nodded. "Ms. Carmichael said I could try taking Minnie out this time — she's supposed to be awesome on the trail."

While the others hurried off to the tack room, Dylan paused in front of Morello's stall. As soon as he saw her, the pony came up and started nosing her pockets for treats.

She laughed and pushed him away. "If I couldn't even remember my clothes, what makes you think I have any treats for you?" she joked. But when he nudged at her jacket pocket, she stuck her hand in to check — and brought out a couple of peppermints. "Well, what do you know," she said, feeding them to the pony. "I guess Honey is prepared for anything."

Glancing up, she saw that Honey and Lani were already returning from the tack room with their saddles. "Get a move on, Walsh," Lani ordered. "We've got a lot of riding to do."

"Aye-aye, captain." Dylan hurried down the aisle to the tack room. Inside she found Malory perched on a stool attaching a new rubber band to one of the safety stirrups on Tybalt's saddle. "Hey," Dylan greeted her, realizing the two of them hadn't really talked since the dance. "How are you doing?"

"Okay," Malory replied.

Dylan peered into her face, trying to read her expression. She'd been so busy panicking over Ali since waking up that she realized she'd barely thought about Malory's traumatic time the previous evening. "Really?" she said. "Have you heard from Caleb since — you know — last night?"

"No." Malory bit her lip and glanced down at the saddle on her lap. "But I'm not sure that's a bad thing."

"What do you mean?"

"You heard him last night." Malory finally looked up and met her eye. "All that talk about winning . . . I just don't think that winning ribbons is everything. Look at today — it feels like we just won Olympic gold, and there isn't a ribbon or trophy in sight!"

"Well, actually . . ." Dylan gestured toward the trophy case visible in the hallway nearby.

Malory smiled. "You know what I mean."

"Okay, but how can you be so calm about this?" Dylan asked. "I would think that after last night . . ."

"I know." Malory sighed and rubbed at a spot of dust on the saddle. "I guess I've had the chance to think it through. And I just want to make sure I really know Caleb before things go any further. No more surprises."

"Oh." Dylan wasn't sure what to think about that. But she'd just remembered another piece of unfinished business. "By the way, Mal," she said, "I need to apologize to you."

"You do? For what?" Malory had already returned her attention to her stirrup. "Have you finally realized I was right yesterday when I said blue eye shadow looks terrible on me?"

"No, I'll never agree with that," Dylan joked weakly, feeling nervous about what she needed to say next. "I want to say I'm sorry for suspecting your motives this past week — you know, with the Lynsey thing and all. Accusing you of turning against Ali, and worse yet, that thing about becoming Lynsey's BFF." Dylan mocked herself by making quote marks in the air with her fingers. "I was being crazy. Obviously. I know you'd never do something like that."

Malory looked uncertain for a moment. Then she laughed. "Yeah," she said. "You *are* crazy. But that's one of the best things about you."

Dylan grinned, relieved. "That's what everybody says. I'm just lucky you're so darn sane to make up for it."

"Absolutely." Malory grinned back, hoisting her saddle onto her hip and standing up. "That's what makes us such a great team."

FOR MALORY,
JOINING AN ELITE
RIDING TEAM COMES
WITH HURDLES.

Chestnut Hill #6

by LAUREN BROOKE
Author of the HEARTLAND series

MALORY HAS A NATURAL GIFT FOR RIDING, so
it's no surprise when she's invited to try out
for an exclusive summer riding team. But
to get in the game, she needs to find a horse
to ride, compete against her classmates for
a spot, and deal with the nerve-racking fact
that Caleb—the boy she's liked all year—will
be trying out too.

■SCHOLASTIC

www.scholastic.com/chestnuthill   CH6T

Girls Rule These Series!

UNDERCOVER GIRL

by Christine Harris

Jesse Sharpe is an orphan, a genius, and a secret agent. She trails suspects, cracks codes, and kicks butt in a world where she can trust no one but herself.

The AMAZING DAYS of ABBY HAYES®

by Anne Mazer

In a family of superstars, it's hard to stand out. But Abby is about to surprise her friends, her family, and most of all, herself!

www.scholastic.com/abbyhayes

DEAR DUMB DIARY,

by Jim Benton

In Jamie Kelly's hilarious, candid (and sometimes not-so-nice) diaries, she promises everything she writes is true... or at least as true as it needs to be.

www.scholastic.com/deardumbdiary

■SCHOLASTIC